Fairytale
Christmas
on the Island

De-ann Black

Paperback edition published 2023

Fairytale Christmas on the Island

ISBN: 9798867925369

Fairytale Christmas on the Island is the fourth book in the Scottish Highlands & Island Romance series.

Also by De-ann Black (Romance, Action/Thrillers & Children's books). See her Amazon Author page or website for further details about her books, screenplays, illustrations and artwork. www.De-annBlack.com

Action/Thrillers:
Knight in Miami.
Agency Agenda.
Love Him Forever.
Someone Worse.
Electric Shadows.
The Strife of Riley.
Shadows of Murder.

Romance:
Christmas Weddings
Fairytale Christmas on the Island
The Cure for Love at Christmas
Vintage Dress Shop on the Island
Scottish Island Fairytale Castle
Scottish Loch Summer Romance
Scottish Island Knitting Bee
Sewing & Mending Cottage
Knitting Shop by the Sea
Colouring Book Cottage
Knitting Cottage
Oops! I'm the Paparazzi, Again
The Bitch-Proof Wedding
Embroidery Cottage
The Dressmaker's Cottage
The Sewing Shop
Heather Park
The Tea Shop by the Sea
The Bookshop by the Seaside
The Sewing Bee
The Quilting Bee

Snow Bells Wedding
Snow Bells Christmas
Summer Sewing Bee
The Chocolatier's Cottage
Christmas Cake Chateau
The Beemaster's Cottage
The Sewing Bee By The Sea
The Flower Hunter's Cottage
The Christmas Knitting Bee
The Sewing Bee & Afternoon Tea
Shed In The City
The Bakery By The Seaside
The Christmas Chocolatier
The Christmas Tea Shop & Bakery
The Bitch-Proof Suit

Colouring books:
Summer Nature. Flower Nature. Summer Garden. Spring Garden. Autumn Garden. Sea Dream. Festive Christmas. Christmas Garden. Flower Bee. Wild Garden. Flower Hunter. Stargazer Space. Christmas Theme. Faerie Garden Spring. Scottish Garden Seasons. Bee Garden.

Embroidery books:
Floral Garden Embroidery Patterns
Floral Spring Embroidery Patterns
Christmas & Winter Embroidery Patterns
Floral Nature Embroidery Designs
Scottish Garden Embroidery Designs

Contents

CHAPTER ONE

The winter sky in the late afternoon cast the Scottish island's small town in a twilight glow. The sea along the coast shimmered like liquid silver, and a few boats bobbed gently in the little harbour.

The beautiful island was situated off the west coast of Scotland where the nearest city was Glasgow, and regular ferries sailed back and forth from the mainland, barely twenty miles away.

The shops along the main street glowed with lights and Christmas decorations, including the cake shop with its delicious array of cakes with fondant icing and a selection of chocolatier sweet temptations. The shop was owned by Innis.

Innis was considered to be the most handsome man on the island. And there were a fair few other men worthy of that title. But there was something about Innis that set him apart including his dark brooding looks and amber eyes — wolf eyes, that set many a woman's heart fluttering.

Fairy lights stretched along the main street beside the harbour, and a large Christmas tree shone in the heart of the town. Winters were wonderful and white Christmases were guaranteed, with the green and heather covered hills rising up from the coast glistening with snow and ice crystals. It hadn't snowed yet, but there was a sense of snow in the clear, crisp air.

Shops, restaurants, a tea shop and cafe bars followed the curve of the bay, and cottages and

1

farmhouses were dotted across the countryside that rose up from the coast to forests of thick greenery and fields.

The turrets of the magnificent castle, known locally as the fairytale castle, were silhouetted against the darkening sky. Barely a five minute drive from the main street, the castle was set in a large estate, and was now a successful hotel catering to guests wanting a holiday break in a fairytale location. Parties and special functions were part of the castle's weekly entertainments, available to guests, visitors to the island and those living locally.

Owned by the local laird, the running of the castle had been left in the capable hands of his three sons, all in their early thirties, while the laird and his wife spent time on the mainland on their travels and business. They'd been away for a few seasons now, and had no plans to return before the New Year.

Finlay, the oldest, was happy to take on the laird's tasks, assisted by his younger brother, Ean. The middle brother, Innis, helped them too, while running his cake shop in the main street and using the castle's large, well–equipped kitchen to create his chocolate confectionery. All three brothers were rich, handsome and single, though Finlay and Ean had girlfriends that they were planning to marry in the not too distant future.

In the wintry glow, Innis was lit up in the window of his cake shop, putting fairy lights around the edges to highlight the cakes and chocolates on display. He wore his chef's collarless, short–sleeve white shirt and black trousers that unintentionally emphasised his fit physique.

Those wolf eyes saw Skye walking by the window. Beautiful Skye, the one woman constantly on his mind these days, though being away on business trips to the mainland recently had thwarted his hopes of taking their friendship further. Skye had been away too. After the fashion show at the castle, the success of it had brought in more offers of modelling work that she'd accepted. Work and circumstances had kept them apart as autumn had become winter, and now that the festive season was upon them, his schedule was set to become even busier.

But still...there she was. Her long, strawberry blonde hair was pinned up in messy pleats, and the dark velvet trousers she wore emphasised her long, lithe legs and slender but shapely figure. A pink jumper she'd knitted herself was fashionably cropped and those soft lips of hers smiled at him as she went by, admired his light display and gave him a cheery thumbs up.

Taken off–guard by the effect she had on him, he wasn't sure if he'd smiled at her. If anyone could break through his serious mien, it was Skye and her cheerful attitude.

Skye breezed into the cake shop to collect the order she'd placed for a dozen iced doughnuts with chocolate sprinkles. The decor of the shop was as pretty as the frontage. Pale pink and vanilla yellow, with touches of strawberry, lemon and cream, created a colour scheme that was light and airy.

Innis' skills as an artisan baker were on full view. Glass display cabinets were filled with a tempting selection of cakes, all lit with spotlights. His chocolates and confectionary merited the cabinet they had to themselves. Boxes of his luxury chocolates sat on a shelf behind the counter. Skye had enjoyed his chocolates, from truffles to fondant creams, though she'd yet to taste his latest festive chocolatier range that included added spices and white chocolate sprinkled like snow across the toffee cups.

The doughnuts were Skye's contribution to the local knitting bee night that was being held that evening in the knitting shop next door to the cake shop. Skye and her sister Holly owned the vintage dress shop two doors down, and modelled part–time. In her late twenties, Skye was slightly younger than Holly. When Skye and Innis were both on the island, their paths regularly crossed. She'd been attracted to Innis for a while, but suspected the feeling wasn't mutual....until fairly recently during the fashion show at the castle where Innis made her believe otherwise.

There had been a time when Innis wasn't sure about his feelings for the mercurial and light–hearted Skye, but that time was long gone. They were complete opposites, but he believed that added to their attraction to each other. Since earlier in the year, he'd been feeling different about his priorities, and a deep longing to settle down and find love and happiness had stalked his senses. Some days it gnawed at his core, urging him to find what was clearly missing in his life — true love.

4

Rosabel and Primrose, the two assistants working in the cake shop, smiled when Skye walked up to the counter. Both in their latter years, they'd come out of retirement to work for Innis. They'd owned their own bakery business using secret family recipes. When Innis offered to pay them for the use of the recipes in his new cake shop, they'd accepted his offer but wanted to work for him as part of the deal. Flexible hours were agreed, and since they'd started working for him at the cake shop, his business had thrived, and so had the two sisters.

Rosabel wore a pink apron, while Primrose opted for pale yellow, and pretty bakery caps contained their silvery curls with only a few random curls peeking out. The flexible hours they worked at the cake shop allowed them to do what they loved — bake cakes, while enjoying chatting to customers and the buzz of the baking business.

Innis had taken a chance on hiring them, but now, he couldn't think of anyone more capable to run the shop while he was away on business. He was planning to expand his range of chocolates and had been away attending courses and meetings with chocolate suppliers on the mainland, in Glasgow, Edinburgh and London. His chocolatier work was something he wanted to emphasise in the cake shop, and boxes of his luxury chocolates were lit up in the window display along with the cakes.

'I've got your order ready,' Rosabel said to Skye, lifting a box of doughnuts she'd packed and put it on the counter along with a bag of chocolate scones, a favourite with customers.

'Are you going to the knitting bee tonight?' Skye said to them.

'Yes, we'll be there,' Primrose told her. 'Elspeth is continuing to run the knitting bee nights during the busy festive season, and is encouraging us to make gifts from various crafts, and knit items suitable for winter.'

Elspeth now co–owned the knitting shop along with her aunt Morven, and the bee nights were held weekly from around seven in the evening until nine. Extra evenings were often organised for special events or when more time was needed for the members to help each other with their knitting, sewing, quilting and crafts. Knitting was the mainstay of the bee, but other crafts, especially all forms of sewing and dressmaking, were part of the bee nights.

In her early thirties, Elspeth had agreed to look after her aunt Morven's knitting shop while Morven was away gallivanting on the mainland, as she called it, with her boyfriend, Donall. He was fairly wealthy and part owner of a whisky distillery and two pubs on the island. Now Elspeth had moved permanently from Glasgow to work at the knitting shop, and stayed in the accommodation above the shop with her aunt.

Morven and her new boyfriend, Donall, were in their fifties and had been dating and going on holiday to the mainland recently. Elspeth had come over from Glasgow to run the knitting shop while Morven was away, and ended up falling in love with life on the island — and with Brodrick, owner of the cafe bar next door to the knitting shop. Sandwiched between the cafe bar and the cake shop, Elspeth was often tempted by the delicious aroma of fresh baking and savoury treats from both establishments.

There was talk that Brodrick planned to propose to Elspeth in December, a Christmas engagement, but she wasn't getting her hopes up. Brodrick wanted to whisk Elspeth off to the mainland in the New Year for something special, and she sensed he was planning to pop the question then.

Skye paid for the cakes and scones. Tea and cakes were served at the knitting bee, and members often contributed to the tasty treats.

'We'll see you and Holly later at the bee,' Primrose said to Skye.

Rosabel glanced over at Innis wondering if he'd take the hint that Skye was leaving and perhaps try to engage her in conversation.

Primrose and Rosabel had noticed the widening gap between Innis and Skye. They'd had such high hopes of a romance between the two of them, especially as Innis had showed how much he liked Skye at the fashion show. But since then...work and more work along with separations had broken that brief bond of closeness. There had been no chance to build on it, and rather like the autumn, the vibrancy had faded and was now at the mercy of a stark winter.

Skye smiled at Primrose and Rosabel and then walked out of the shop with a glance at Innis working on finishing the light display.

Rosabel let out an exasperated sigh, directed at Innis and his behaviour.

He'd been on the receiving end of it before and looked over, knowing exactly what she meant.

Rosabel shook her head at him.

Primrose spoke up. Her words didn't miss him and hit the wall. 'You're letting a lovely young woman slip through your fingers. Sometimes I despair at your attitude, Innis.'

He didn't balk at the rebuke, mainly because he agreed.

'Some other man is going to step in and invite Skye to the Christmas parties and events on the island,' Rosabel warned him.

He agreed with this as well. He paused for a second, then selected a large box of his special Christmas chocolates from the window display, and hurried after her.

She'd stopped to admire the yarn in the window of the pretty pink knitting shop and then walked on past Brodrick's cafe bar towards the vintage dress shop.

'Skye!' His rich, deep voice resonated in the cold air.

She stopped and glanced back at him, watching him striding towards her. His handsome face was highlighted in the glow of the lights from the shops, but his expression was serious. A look she'd become accustomed to. The man who rationed his smiles. But when he let one escape from his sensual lips, his sexy smile set her heart alight.

She sighed inwardly.

A broken heart was the last thing she needed, and she refused to put herself in jeopardy. Being within breathing distance of a man like Innis was foolhardy unless she felt it was worth the risk. Some days she didn't. Some nights she did. Her mercurial nature worked for and against her. No outright winner now. Seeing Innis hurrying after her carrying a box of chocolates weakened her resolve. So. Be. It.

'Yes,' she said brightly. 'Is something wrong?'

'No, nothing,' he lied. Everything was wrong when it came to him and romance.

Her beautiful, wide blue eyes with their curious upswept tilt looked up at him. She was fairly tall, but he still towered over her. She sensed he was telling a fib.

Before she could decide why he'd run after her, he thrust the box of chocolate at her.

'For the knitting bee night,' he said.

'Oh, thank you. That's very kind. The ladies will enjoy these.' She tried not to look at the lean muscles in his bare forearms or show the effect his tall, broad–shouldered build had on her.

'They're my latest selection.'

'I hear you've been away a lot recently, on your chocolatier work.'

'I have. To Glasgow, Edinburgh, London, it's taken up my time. Fortunately, Rosabel and Primrose have held the fort, and my brothers too. But I'm back now for the festive season and throughout the New Year.'

She nodded, taking this in. Taking him in. All hint of his summer tan had faded with the autumn and now his handsome features had a quality as cold as sculptured ice.

'You and Holly have been away too.' He filled the gap she'd left. 'Modelling I believe.'

'Yes, after the fashion show offers of modelling work came in, and we split the jobs so that one of us was left here to run our shop.' It had been the first fashion show on the island, and the castle's ballroom size function room had been the perfect setting for it.

'Are you home now for Christmas?'

He was making small talk? 'We are. No more gadding off to model on the mainland.' A look of excitement lit up her face. 'I'm looking forward to Christmas. I love it. It's our first Christmas running our dress shop.'

They'd taken over the shop earlier in the year when their mother retired due to wanting to spend more leisure time with their father and travelling. Skye and Holly had been living and working on the mainland in the fashion industry, including modelling work, for a few years. But they'd jumped at the chance to move to the island from the city and had built up the vintage dress shop. They'd widened the stock to include tartan vintage dresses that had caused quite a stir of excitement at the fashion show.

The dresses in their shop ranged from designer pieces from decades past to off–the–peg, pre–loved dresses from yesteryear.

They'd restored the original sign across the frontage — *the vintage dress shop*.

Skye's old–fashioned pink bicycle often sat outside the shop, not only as part of the styling, but for her personal use when she popped to the post office with the orders for customers even though they had a car. Or times when she loved cycling along the coast and letting the sea breeze blow through her hair.

Their online sales had soared in the past few months, and they'd made a success of the shop by focussing on vintage dress fashions galore. They had reliable suppliers, and both Skye and Holly were skilled at sewing, repairing and upgrading the older designs, making them seem like new.

Local sales accounted for a fair amount of their revenue, but their main profit came from sales far and wide via their website. Skye had plans to extend the range and work to highlight the seasons. The Christmas party season was on show in the front window with the three mannequins wearing head to toe festive glamorous gowns that sparkled almost as much as the fairy lights inside and outside the dress shop. Maybe she'd overdone the lights, but then again, you could never have too much sparkle when it came to Christmas — and party dresses.

Innis' comment pulled her back from her wayward thoughts. 'You were the first shop to put your decorations up.'

She laughed. 'Ah, you noticed.'

'Those lights are hard to miss, even from the mainland.'

He'd made a joke. She smiled at him.

Another pause, not awkward, just lingering.

She decided to ask him if the fairytale ball gossip was true. 'I've heard that a ball is being held this Christmas at the castle. You know what the local gossip is like, but it would be great if it was true. I've always wanted to attend a fancy ball at a castle and sweep around the dance floor dressed like a princess.'

Her words hung in the cold air for a moment, and she saw his eyes darken to molten amber.

He chose his words carefully as he replied. 'Finlay, Ean and I have tentatively discussed it, but we won't decide until our final meeting tonight.' He explained the main drawbacks. 'We have various party events on the run–up to Christmas, culminating in the Christmas Eve dinner dance in the main function room. It's become a tradition. Guests and local people expect the dinner dance. With my parents being away, they're leaving the decision to us.'

Skye nodded. 'So you don't want to change the traditional dinner dance.'

'The meal, the dinner, is the main attraction, and our chefs have been hard at work preparing the menus. We could, of course, use the dinner as part of the ball, but then there's the issue of guests having to wear ball gowns and evening suits. It's extra expense for guests. A proper ball, a fairytale ball, merits that everyone dresses accordingly, otherwise it's just the Christmas dinner dance by another name.'

'Yes, I see what you mean...' the disappointment sounded in her voice, even though she tried to hide it.

'Finlay has attended a few balls and says that the level of opulence raises the bar fairly high.'

'But surely your large function room is as beautiful as any ballroom, especially with the lovely decor and chandeliers,' she reasoned.

'It is, but it would still require those attending to turn up in full ballroom attire. It's a bit of a tall order for people thinking they could wear a smart suit or a pretty evening or cocktail dress.'

She sighed wearily. 'That sounds like a no–go then. But that's the trouble with local gossip. It spreads like wildfire and gathers all sorts of false speculation.'

For a moment, Innis pictured Skye wearing a sparkling ball gown and his heart thundered in his chest at the thought of it.

'The main reason I'm asking is that Holly and I have been offered a load of gorgeous vintage ball gowns by one of our suppliers. We could accept and sell the dresses online, but it would've been handy to make them available to the local ladies. I've only ever worn ball gowns for fashion shows and modelling photo–shoots, and the dresses felt extra special.'

He hated disappointing her.

'Don't frown or fret. It's fine. The Christmas dinner dance sounds wonderful, and we offer lovely evening dresses in our shop.'

He nodded dolefully and the muscles in his firm jaw tightened, holding back all the things he wanted to say to her. How he'd missed her, wished he hadn't been away on business, and that things could be different between them. Closer. Much closer. Instead, he felt his reply had pushed her away.

She brightened up. 'Thanks again for the chocolates. I felt that Holly and I should bring plenty of sweet sustenance to the knitting bee tonight. We're making loads of Christmas pressies. And I'm knitting a jumper that I've almost finished. It's like this one I'm wearing, only in Christmassy red.'

'It's beautiful.' His deep voice said so much more than compliment her hand knitted jumper.

A blush rose up across her lovely pale complexion, but failed to reach full warmth due to the cold breeze now sweeping in from the sea.

'I won't keep you standing here in the cold,' he said, seeing her try not to shiver.

With her arms filled with the cakes, scones and box of chocolates, she smiled sweetly and hurried on to her shop, nudging the door open and disappearing inside.

'What was Innis saying to you?' Holly said, having been peering at them from the dress shop window. She swept her shoulder–length, shiny chestnut hair back from her lovely pale features, and her green eyes widened. 'Was he giving you a box of chocolates, inviting you out on a date, or both?'

'Just the chocolates for the knitting bee. I'm okay with that.' Skye put the cake shop items down on the shop counter.

'What? You wouldn't want Innis to ask you out on a date? I know that's not true.' Wearing a green velvet midi dress, a throwback to the seventies, and dark emerald tights with black pumps, Holly stepped away from the window.

'He's a heartbreaker,' said Skye. 'And yes, I've liked him for a while now, but I want to enjoy Christmas. Our first Christmas owning and running our shop. Romance, especially with a man like Innis, could skew everything.'

'What about that night at the fashion show? He walked down the runway with you. Everyone saw how much he liked you.'

'But nothing happened. He didn't follow through by asking me out for dinner or a date. It was like we rattled back down to where we were before the show. Circling around each other.'

Holly reconsidered. 'Maybe you're right. Innis would be hard work. Unless he was madly and deeply in love with you, which I'm prepared to believe...but...he needs to show you that he cares. If not, then you're right. Be socially polite to him, but accept other offers for dinner dates.'

Skye looked thoughtful.

'I know you've had offers,' Holly told her.

'So have you.'

'Yes, but no one I'm interested in.' Holly wished it was otherwise, but there was no one she'd felt that special spark with.

'What about Lyle? You'd never be short on being plied with cakes and whatever else he has on offer in his tea shop.'

Holly shook her head. 'Lyle is an acquired taste, unlike his cakes.'

'His cousin, Rory?' Skye threw another name into the romance ring.

'Rory is happily dating Rowen.'

Skye pressed her lips together and nodded, now running out of viable options.

Holly shrugged. 'Perhaps I'll meet my perfect Christmas match at one of the castle functions.'

'A mystery man, waiting in the wings, ready to step out into the spotlight and steal your heart away.'

'Did you ask Innis if they're holding a ball at the castle this year? Or is it just a rumour?'

'I asked him. He said he's having a meeting, again, with his brothers tonight to make a final decision. And then listed the reasons for it being a thumbs down.'

Holly gestured to the computer screen, reminding her of the number of ball gowns from one of their suppliers that were on offer.

'It's tempting to say yes, and then worry about selling them to customers,' said Skye.

'Are you kidding me? These will sell like hot Christmas pies. I'll buy one of them if the ball gets a thumbs up.'

Skye stepped closer and peered at the pictures of the dresses listed. 'I've been trying not to look at them, especially that pale pink sparkly ball gown.' Skye loved pink, and she'd worn a pink satin ball gown to a previous event, but this dress...wow! It was layers of pink organza sprinkled with sparkle, her perfect fairytale ball gown.

'They're designer dresses from the fifties,' Holly said, offering encouragement. 'That pink dress would make you look like a fairytale princess at the ball.'

'It's a real bargain. The sequins and crystals need securing and I could add some new ones on the bodice...' Skye pictured how she'd rescue the dress and bring it back to how it looked in its heyday.

'Let's make a deal,' Holly said, sounding as usual like the sensible one. 'We'll go to the knitting bee, discuss the local gossip, knit, chat, eat cake, and the evening will fly in. Then tomorrow we'll find out if there's going to be a ball at the castle this year. If there is, we'll invest in buying the ball gowns, and if not, we'll suck up our bitter disappointment, forgo the dresses, and drown our sorrows in hot chocolate with extra sprinkles. The latter always helps.'

Skye nodded firmly. She pushed her palm towards the screen. 'Take the temptation away until we know what Innis and his brothers have decided.'

Holly clicked the list off and instead showed Skye the online orders for dresses that had come in during the afternoon. 'Want to pack a few before we get ready for the bee?'

'Okay. We could still make it in time to take them to the post office.'

In a flurry of chiffon, tulle, tartan and silk, they wrapped up the orders, and then Skye jumped on her pink bicycle and pedalled like blazes to the post office along the harbour. The bike's front and rear baskets were stuffed full. She made the collection that was due to be loaded on to the ferry by a whisker and with the help of the postmaster.

The early twilight sky glistened with stars as she pedalled back calmly to the dress shop. The clear night skies were something she adored about living on the island.

And there was the North Star shining brightest in the vast sky.

Come on, she wished upon the star. Agree to hold a ball at the castle. She pictured Innis, Finlay and Ean discussing this later and put all the positive vibes she could muster into her wish. She didn't make wishes very often, but when she did, she gave it her all. Few, if any, of her special wishes ever came true. But there was always hope.

CHAPTER TWO

Innis locked his cake shop up for the night. He'd left the Christmas lights on along with a few spotlights that illuminated the cakes and chocolates on display. Beautifully iced cakes decorated with flowers made from fondant icing had festive bows tied around them. Some were traditional fruit cakes while others were vanilla sponges filled with buttercream, and strawberry cakes. Glacé fruit cupcakes were popular for Christmas and the red and green cherries and other fruits glistened under the lights. His chocolate Yule logs were rich with chocolate icing and decorated with fondant holly.

The cake shop exterior was painted pale vanilla with touches of soft pink, creating a pretty pastel look. Hanging baskets were filled with flowers during the warmer months, but were taken down in the winter and lanterns were hung up that gave a welcoming glow to the shop.

He got into his car and drove off, glancing at the knitting shop lit up and sensing the buzz of activity at the back of the shop where the bee nights were held. Skye would be there.

It was after seven o'clock and he'd worked late baking cakes for the following day and inevitable early start. Fortunately, he loved baking and making chocolates so he felt no hardship in his schedule.

Often he liked to walk up to the highest hill after closing the cake shop to admire the view of the small town and distant villages along the coast and glistening sea. The fairytale castle and its estate, that included thistle loch and forget–me–not waterfall, could be viewed from the hilltop. Lights from the outlying islands twinkled far off in the distance. The golden hour skies with their amber, pink and lilac glow created mellow twilights where he enjoyed unwinding before heading home to the castle. He could've done with this tonight, to think what he wanted to do regarding Skye. But there was no time to meander up into the hills.

Driving home to the castle along the coast road, he thought about the meeting he had that evening with his brothers to decide about the ball. Skye's comments replayed in his mind, and the way her trusting blue eyes had looked at him, hopeful that there would be a Christmas ball, made his heart ache. Instead of time easing the intensity of his feelings for her, the past few weeks of being separated due to work had increased his longing to be with her.

Glancing out the window, the shimmering flat calm of the silvery sea made the outlying islands look so far away. They were part of the reason why the island enjoyed a temperate climate, sheltering it from the fierce winds and rain. Mild springs and warm summers were followed by glorious autumn days, before the winter kicked in. Frosty days at best. Rainstorms at their worst. Smirry rain that blanketed the coast in ethereal grey mist, and hailstones that penetrated everything except the depths of the forests. The warrior trees, as they were known, the tall, dark pines around the edges of the castle gardens, looked like silhouettes of ancient warriors guarding the castle from invaders, shielding the castle from the worst of the rain.

But nothing could shield the island, or the castle, from the depths of the winter snow. Plenty of snow fell throughout December and January, ensuring a winter wonderland for the festive season.

Once the first flurry sprinkled the island with a light dusting of flakes, it was a whiteout all the way to the New Year and beyond. Rain would inevitably dent the white perfection when it dowsed the land in torrents, but the snow soon filled in the gaps, resulting again in the perfect festive snow scene.

Heading away from the coast and up into the depths of the forest road that led to the castle's estate, he wondered if he should forgo getting involved with Skye. His feelings already ran deeper than he'd ever felt, and seemed to build as time went on. Seeing her earlier made him want to ask her to have dinner with him...and take it from there. He knew where it would lead him. He thought he knew where it would lead her. And that was the problem. *Don't break her heart* was a warning issued to him throughout his adult life when it came to dating.

He wasn't the type to flirt and play around a lot. But he'd unintentionally broken a fair few hearts, and had his broken once three years ago by a woman he thought he could trust, until she cheated on him then upped and left him and went home to the city, citing that island life, especially with him, wasn't for her. His heart had mended and he realised that his ex–girlfriend hadn't been the one for him.

But where did that leave Skye? And him?

He shrugged off his doubts and inner turmoil as he drove up to the castle that was bordered by the warrior trees silhouetted against the wintry night sky filled with stars.

The fairytale castle glowed with lights and activity. A festive dinner was being held for guests in the function room. Lit with chandeliers, it had an expensive ballroom quality to it.

Hurrying past reception and side–stepping guests milling around and heading in for dinner, he ran up the private staircase that led to his suite of rooms that he called home. Along the hallway on the same upper floor, Finlay and Ean lived too, with Ean housed at the back of the castle, while Finlay and Innis had a view of the coast and the sea from their windows at the front of the castle. Finlay had the added benefit of access to one of the turrets. The other turret was part of his parents' accommodation.

The castle's decor was stylish, tastefully designed, with plush tartan carpeting in shades of dark grey and black. Oak beams were set against the white and beige walls, and table lamps created a welcoming glow.

Paintings depicting the castle and estate hung on the walls. The countryside and seascapes in both oils and watercolours dated back to the original pieces owned by the castle, but other recent work, including those painted by Ean, brought touches of modern classic art to the decor.

Innis' private quarters consisted of luxury furnishings in shades of winter grey, white and beige. The living room had a plush, pale grey carpet, stylish couch and chairs, an oak desk where he kept his silver laptop and business paperwork, wall–mounted television, and lamps strategically placed to create a relaxing ambiance.

The view from the window stretched all the way from the gardens at the front of the castle to the sea and distant islands way beyond. He liked to look out at it at the end of a hectic day, or when his thoughts troubled him. It was a well–used view.

A door led through to the bedroom with its en suite bathroom, both sizeable and luxurious. Grey silk sheets adorned his double bed, and antique style wardrobes housed his plentiful suits and expensive casual wear.

His kilts and accoutrements including two sporrans — one with a silver chain, were kept in a separate wardrobe. He had ghillie shirts in white, cream and black that laced up the front to reveal his strong chest. There were other dress shirts, waistcoats and cropped jackets, and skean dhus that tucked into his thick woollen socks.

Innis changed out of his chef's baking attire and into expensive trousers, shirt and tie. Often he'd wear his kilt, especially for the ceilidh nights, but this evening his suited look was fine. With guests being in the castle on a permanent basis, Innis and his brothers didn't do casual when it came to clothes. They dressed well whenever they were likely to encounter the guests, particularly in the evenings for dinner and parties.

He looked at himself in the mirror as he straightened his grey silk tie — and thought about Skye. Yes, the problem was *he liked Skye*, really liked

22

her. She was a lovely, kind, sweet, fun–loving, hardworking and beautiful young woman.

The warning played again in his thoughts.

Don't break her heart...

'A box of luxury chocolates!' Elspeth exclaimed as the tea was being made in the knitting shop's small kitchen area. The room at the back of the knitting shop was set up with tables and chairs for the knitting bee night. The patio doors leading on to the garden were closed to keep the room cosy. 'Is Innis trying to sweeten us up?'

Elspeth wore her blonde hair in a neat ponytail, and her trim figure suited the blue jeans and white jumper she was wearing. Her Aunt Morven was at a whisky tasting evening with her boyfriend, Donall. But there were plenty of bee members to help set up the tables and chairs for the knitting bee, and make the tea. Everyone joined in and there was always a happy and lively atmosphere with lots of knitting and crafting along with the tea and chatter.

'Innis can ply me with chocolates all he wants.' Rowen picked a chocolate truffle and popped it in her mouth. Her long red hair hung in silky waves around her shoulders and her pale complexion and green eyes suited the lilac, hand–knitted jumper she was wearing. She'd been dating Rory, a local builder in his late twenties, since they'd both taken part in the fashion show. Neither of them had experience in modelling, but they made an attractive young couple, and had been dating since that night.

The knitting bee members shared their skills and craft items — everything from new yarn to fabric for quilting, and patterns and techniques.

Elspeth and her Aunt Morven lived above the shop in the converted two–storey property. The shop stocked an extensive range of yarns, knitting needles and other haberdashery accessories. Like her aunt, Elspeth was an expert knitter, but the bee nights had encouraged her to get back into sewing, quilting and dressmaking.

Knitting jumpers, hats and scarves for the winter were a popular choice during the evening.

Rowen had brought along samples of her new yarn. She spun her own range of yarn that she sold from home and in the knitting shop. The samples were enough to try out the texture and quality of the double–knitting yarn.

Ailsa came hurrying in. 'Sorry I'm late. I was dealing with orders at my shop.' Ailsa owned the local craft shop nearby, and modelled knitwear and fashion part–time to boost her shop earnings. She had a long, dark bob, a lovely pale complexion and azure blue eyes. Ean had been in love with her for a while and she'd recently started dating him. She shrugged her coat off and hung it over the back of her chair, flopping down, and pulling the embroidery she was working on from her craft bag.

Rosabel and Primrose carried two trays of tea and cakes through and sat them down for the ladies to help themselves.

Primrose had been knitting a Fair Isle jumper. 'I usually have my winter jumpers knitted by now, but we've been so busy this past wee while looking after the cake shop while Innis was away. Not that I'm complaining. We ran our own bakery shop for over thirty years, so it was fun running the shop by ourselves.'

'We even added a couple of our secret recipes, ones that even Innis doesn't know about, to the cakes on offer,' said Rosabel. 'Customers liked them.'

Skye helped serve the cakes and chocolate scones she'd contributed, while other ladies had brought home baking to the bee.

'I heard that Innis ran after you with the box of chocolates,' Nettie said to Skye. In her forties, Nettie was knitting a jumper for her husband Shuggie, a local taxi driver.

'He said the chocolates were for the knitting bee night,' Skye explained. 'They're his latest selection. I think he's looking for feedback, so remember to tell him if you like them when you're in his cake shop.'

'Did he ask you out?' Rosabel said to Skye, eager to know what happened between the two of them.

'No!' Skye fussed with the tea and cakes and tried not to blush. 'Nothing like that.'

Primrose frowned. 'He ran after you fast enough.'

'Well, he didn't even hint at asking me out,' said Skye.

'What happened between the two of you?' Nettie said to Skye. 'It was obvious he had a fancy for you at the fashion show.'

'Nothing happened,' Skye told her. 'After the show Holly and I had invited some of our friends who'd attended the show to come back to our house for a girls' night, a sleepover. We'd promised them we'd do that, so I couldn't waltz off with Innis even if I'd wanted to. And then the following day my phone was ringing off the hook and offers for modelling work were coming in.' She sighed and shrugged. 'So I grabbed the chances that were offered. So did Holly.'

'We took it in turns to go away on assignments while one of us stayed to look after the dress shop,' Holly told them.

'Then with Innis being away on his chocolatier business, the closeness was lost,' said Skye. 'And you all know what he's like. Innis isn't one for showing his true feelings unless he's being grumpy. He's quite prickly at times.'

'Take it from us, Skye, he really likes you,' Primrose assured her. 'The two of you just need a chance to get close again.'

'What about the fairytale ball?' said Elspeth. 'Is the gossip true that Innis and his brothers are holding a ball this Christmas at the castle?'

Skye shook her head. 'I asked him, but it doesn't seem likely. He's meeting with Finlay and Ean tonight to discuss it.'

'A ball would be great,' Holly said, looking hopeful. 'We've got the offer of wonderful ball gowns from one of our suppliers. A job lot, so we'd be able to sell them as real bargains.'

'They have this gorgeous pink ball gown,' Skye enthused.

'I've never been to a ball,' Elspeth told them.

None of them had.

Skye picked up the red jumper she was knitting and started working on it while they all chatted.

'How are you and Brodrick getting on? Any hint of an engagement?' Rosabel said to Elspeth.

A blush rose in Elspeth's cheeks. 'No, but we're getting along fine.'

'The two of you really hit it off,' Primrose commented. 'We've been thinking that a Christmas engagement could be in Brodrick's plans.'

'No,' said Elspeth, though she wished this was true. 'Brodrick's been busy with his cafe bar and even busier now during Christmastime.'

Brodrick's cafe bar was next door to the knitting shop, and after the bee nights, Elspeth always popped in for a late night supper with him.

The conversation circled back round to Innis and Skye when a voice interrupted their evening.

'Knock, knock!' Lyle called to them seconds before his cheery face appeared from the front of the shop. 'Can I come in, ladies?'

'Yes, come on in,' said Elspeth.

Lyle owned the popular vintage style tea shop nearby. He was in his late twenties, fairly tall, a fine looking man with light brown hair and hazel eyes with a mischievous twinkle. Having trained as a patisserie chef, he'd taken over the tea shop when his grandparents retired, and so far he'd made a success of it with his new recipes and sheer hard work.

'I come bearing fairy cakes,' Lyle announced. He wore a white shirt, black trousers and a chef's apron, and was carrying a large white box filled with cakes. 'I wanted to ask a favour. These are my new recipes for

Christmas. Would you try them and tell me if you like the flavours? I've added gingerbread spice, apricot brandy and various other festive flavours.'

Elspeth pretended to sigh wearily. 'I suppose we could force ourselves to try your new recipes.'

Giggling, the other ladies joined in the fun and helped themselves to the cakes.

'Was that Innis I overheard you gossiping about when I came in?' said Lyle, determined to hang around.

'We were just talking about him and Skye,' said Rosabel. 'We're hoping he'll ask Skye out on a date.'

'Rosabel!' Skye playfully scolded her.

'Well, it's true,' Rosabel insisted. 'We think he's too stubborn to ask her out and needs some encouragement.'

'It's a tricky situation,' said Lyle. 'We think—'

'We?' Skye cut–in.

'Yes, me, Rory, Brodrick, Shuggie, and a few other men,' Lyle explained.

The women looked surprised.

'Don't look so surprised,' Lyle told them. 'We gossip as much as you lot do.'

'So what do you think?' Skye prompted him.

Lyle saw a light flash outside in the back garden, but distracted the women with his conversation, hoping they hadn't noticed it.

'Well...' Lyle began, 'we think that Innis won't ask Skye out because he likes her.'

Holly frowned. 'That makes no sense.'

Ailsa agreed. 'Why wouldn't he ask her if he likes her?'

'Because he doesn't want to hurt her if things go awry. He could break her heart, and we think he doesn't want to do that,' said Lyle. 'With a man like Innis, it's all or nothing.'

Skye wanted Lyle to clarify. 'You mean...'

Lyle nodded. 'If Innis asks you out to dinner, a romantic dinner date, he's in it for the long haul. No half measures in his world.'

Rosabel and Primrose agreed with this.

'He'd be looking at marriage,' said Primrose.

'We think he's ready to settle down,' Lyle added.

Before they could discuss this further, Rory bounded in, looking fit and strong, all broad shoulders under his denim shirt, and lean–hipped in pale blue denim jeans — and then announced, 'Sorry, knock, knock.'

The women laughed.

'Come away in, Rory,' Elspeth beckoned him.

Rory had pale blue eyes that matched the denim he was wearing, and thick sand–blond hair. His features were as well–defined as his build, a handsome young man with a friendly, quicksilver quality about him.

Slightly taller than his cousin, Lyle, he was in his late twenties, and was a self–employed local builder. He'd recently helped convert Lyle's tea shop, building the upstairs level of the two–storey shop to extend the premises. The work was finished by the autumn, and although the shop had remained open during the upstairs work, Lyle held a special party event to launch the extension and promote his new menus.

'How is the cake tasting going?' Rory tucked his thumbs into the pockets of his jeans and stood there smiling at the ladies.

'Deliciously well,' said Ailsa.

Rory looked at the patio doors and then distracted the ladies by admiring their knitting. 'Nice jumpers you're knitting.'

Lyle gave Rory a secret glance to calm down and not give the game away.

'As we seem to have Lyle and Rory joining us at the bee,' said Elspeth, 'can I offer you both a cup of tea?'

'Yes, thanks,' Rory piped up.

Lyle nudged him.

'But not a cup of your tea, Elspeth,' Rory said quickly, trying to undo his mistake. 'I'd like a cup of Rosabel and Primrose's tea.'

Elspeth's cornflower blue eyes blinked at his comment, and the ladies gave a low gasp.

'Is there something wrong with the pair of you?' Rowen spoke up. 'You're acting very—'

'No, nothing strange about our behaviour,' Lyle cut-in.

'Nope. We're hunky–dory,' Rory added, backing him up. 'We're not up to anything.'

Another scolding glance from Lyle was directed at Rory.

'I'll make my own tea.' Rory went to bound through to the kitchen area.

'No, I'll make you a cup of my tea,' Rosabel insisted, wondering what on earth was wrong with Rory and Lyle tonight.

'Did you see that?' Nettie gasped and pointed towards the garden outside the patio doors. 'There was a flash of lights.'

Lyle jumped in to explain away Nettie's suspicions as other members turned to stare outside. 'I never saw anything and I'm facing the patio doors. And so is Rory and he never saw anything either. Did you?' he prompted Rory.

'I saw nothing,' Rory agreed. 'It was probably just a reflection from all the activity going on in here.'

Seeing nothing untoward, the ladies turned away again and got on with their knitting and enjoying their tea and cake.

Moments later, Lyle caught a glimpse of a light outside. It was there and gone in a second. Smiling tightly, he hissed at Rory standing next to him. 'Do something. Cause a distraction.'

Panic flashed across Rory's face that he was responsible for saving their plan, so he did the only thing that came to mind.

'Oh, would you look at that,' Rory announced to the ladies. 'I've got a dangler.' He tugged at one of the buttons on his denim shirt, causing it to dangle from his cuff. 'Would any of you ladies be able to sew it back on for me?'

There were plenty of helpful takers, including his girlfriend, Rowen.

Without hesitation, Rory unbuttoned his shirt and whipped it off to reveal a lean–muscled physique, honed from his building work. Broad shoulders tapered down to a taut torso.

A gasp rippled through the bee members as Rory stood there for all to see in his tight jeans that emphasised his long legs.

He ran an anxious hand through the front of his blond hair and forced a smile.

'Rory!' Rowen exclaimed. 'You don't need to take your shirt off. I could've sewn the button on your sleeve cuff without you stripping it off.' She looked embarrassed. She knew Rory was a confident man, up for a laugh, easy going, and it's what she liked about him, but this... She shook her head in dismay.

Rosabel popped her head round from making the tea in the kitchen area, wondering what had caused the gasp and giggles. Seeing Rory standing like there, rugged and ready, made her gasp too. And then she laughed.

Before any further chaos erupted, a message came through on Lyle's phone. The relief showed on his face as he read it. He nodded firmly to Rory.

'What's going on with the two of you tonight?' Skye said to them.

'Nothing,' Lyle lied.

'Not a thing,' Rory added.

The men smiled, convincing no one.

CHAPTER THREE

Innis, Finlay and Ean sat at a private table in the far corner of the castle's large function room. A roaring log fire crackled in the hearth, and the huge Christmas tree was aglow with lights and baubles.

Chandeliers cast their glittering light over the dance floor.

Guests were seated at tables around the edges of the dance floor having dinner, and many of them were up dancing.

Innis glanced over at them. The dinner dance was a success, as was usual when it came to the functions they held regularly at the castle.

The three of them had finished their dinner and were still discussing the ball. Finlay wore a white shirt, tie and tailored waistcoat. Ean was smartly dressed in a three–piece suit.

'Why have you changed your mind?' Finlay said to Innis. 'You were set against having a Christmas ball, and now you want us to start planning it.' He leaned back, ready to listen to Innis' explanation.

Finlay was nothing like Innis in looks or outlook. He was blond and handsome with gorgeous light aquamarine blue eyes. Of the three brothers, he'd taken his looks from his father, while Ean's chestnut hair, green eyes and talent for art were inherited from his mother. All three of the brothers were tall, lean, strong and handsome, and recently two of them were lucky in love, finally. Since Finlay met and fell in love with Merrilees, he'd been planning to marry her and settle down. Merrilees, a photo–journalist, had arrived on the island in the summer on an assignment from her newspaper editor in Glasgow to write the features for the paper's magazine supplement. The main feature was about the castle. Originally from the island, she'd now moved there to build a future with Finlay.

Innis gave a considered reply. 'I heard that people were looking forward to having a ball and they hoped that we'd go ahead with it.'

Finlay smiled wryly. 'Would one of those people be Skye?'

'She mentioned it to me when I spoke to her today,' Innis admitted, skirting around the details.

Finlay prompted Innis to elaborate as Ean sat back listening to the events unfold.

'Skye said that her shop had been offered ball gowns to sell. Holly and Skye plan to accept the offer if the ball goes ahead, so there would a local dress shop that would supply fancy ball gowns for those attending the party,' Innis explained.

'Ailsa is hoping we hold a ball here,' Ean added.

Finlay leaned forward. 'So are we all now agreeing to hold a fairytale ball for Christmas?'

'I've always wanted to do it,' said Ean.

Finlay and Ean looked at Innis. At their last meeting, Innis' reluctance dominated the conversation, and they'd rescheduled to decide on the evening of the current dinner dance.

Before Innis could confirm that he was now keen to go ahead with it, Geneen came hurrying towards them from reception looking flustered.

In her fifties, trim and efficient, Geneen was one of the castle's key staff and had worked there for years. She was a member of the knitting bee.

'Sorry to interrupt,' Geneen said to them, 'but I've had a message from Rosabel at the knitting shop bee night. Apparently, Lyle and Rory have joined in this evening.'

Ean frowned. 'Lyle and Rory are at the knitting bee?' He needed clarification.

'Yes,' said Geneen. 'And they're not joining in with the knitting or other crafts.'

'Then what are they doing at the bee?' Finlay said to Geneen.

'Making a nuisance of themselves. Lyle is plying them with cake, which is fine. But Rory...he stripped himself half naked in front of the ladies.'

A look of disbelief was shared between the brothers.

Finlay smiled calmly. 'I doubt that Rory would do that.'

Geneen held up her phone to show them the picture Rosabel had sent along with the message. She didn't say a word. She held it in front of them and waited for their reaction when they saw the strapping, bare–chested builder standing in front of the ladies at the knitting bee.

Ean immediately took out his phone. 'I'll call Ailsa. She said she was going to the knitting bee tonight.'

Geneen clicked her phone off. 'I have to get back to attend to the reception desk.' She hurried away, leaving the men with a mountain of trouble to tackle.

'Ailsa, come on, pick up,' Ean urged her. 'She's not answering her phone.'

Innis stood up. 'I'm driving down to the knitting shop to see what's happening.'

'I'm coming with you,' said Ean.

Innis and Ean hurried out of the function room, leaving Finlay to take care of the dinner dance.

As they walked through the reception Murdo tried to waylay them. Murdo was another key member of staff, a sturdy man in his fifties, a handyman and builder and one of the main assistants at the castle.

Murdo held up his phone. 'Have you seen what's happening with Rory at the bee night?'

Innis kept on walking as he replied. 'We're going to check on it right now.'

Ean and Innis continued on towards the doorway as Merrilees arrived at the castle. In her late twenties with shoulder–length blonde hair and grey eyes, she wore a smart pair of black trousers and a winter jacket that suited her slim figure. Her large shoulder bag was filled with her laptop, camera and files of information for her newspaper journalism work.

Merrilees held her phone showing a copy of the picture Shuggie had given her. 'What's happening at the knitting shop?' Shuggie had picked her up in his taxi when she'd arrived home from Glasgow on the ferry and driven her to the castle. His wife Nettie had sent the picture of Rory to him from the knitting bee.

'Ask Finlay,' Ean advised her. 'He'll explain. Sorry, we have to dash.'

Merrilees nodded and continued into the castle.

Innis and Ean ran outside to Innis' car.

Shuggie, who'd just dropped Merrilees off, held up his phone as he shouted to them out the taxi window. 'Nettie's just sent me a picture of Rory—'

Innis cut–in. 'We're taking care of it.' He jumped into his car and started up the engine, while Ean sat in the passenger seat, still trying to phone Ailsa.

'I'm not missing this,' Shuggie muttered to himself and then drove after them, eager to see what the fuss was, especially as Nettie was there at the knitting bee night.

Fluffy was snuggled up and snoozing on his blanket on the passenger seat. As always, when Nettie was out and he was driving the taxi, he was kitten sitting their black and white cat. Fluffy was more cat now than kitten, but didn't like being left alone in the house so Shuggie took the cat with him. Merrilees always made a fuss of Fluffy on the evenings Shuggie picked her up from the ferry down at the harbour.

'Ailsa still isn't answering her phone,' said Ean as Innis drove with purpose down the coast road and along to the main street. He parked outside his cake shop, and the two of them got out of the car and hurried into the knitting shop, shortly followed by Shuggie.

The sound of laughter and chatter filled the air as Innis and Ean walked through to the back room of the shop where the bee night was buzzing.

Rory was casually putting his shirt back on, clearly in no rush to do so, but he put on a spurt when he saw the brothers standing there looking at him, especially Innis. Those wolf eyes cut through him to the bone.

Before words were exchanged in friendship or as foes, the back garden suddenly glowed like a beacon.

Everyone stopped and stared. The chatter ceased and a sense of awe showed on the numerous faces.

Lyle took charge and opened the patio doors, letting the cold night air rush in. He stepped back and waved Elspeth to come over.

Elspeth's face showed trepidation and wonder, and then she smiled when she saw Brodrick standing in the adjoining garden at the back of his cafe bar. He wore a suit, shirt and tie, and his dark russet hair had been slicked back, emphasising his sculptured features and green eyes. Brodrick was the same height as Innis, and had a commanding presence as he held out his hand, inviting Elspeth to join him.

She stepped outside and saw that his entire garden was ablaze with twinkle lights that created a fairytale setting — for his proposal.

Rory had helped him set up the lights, like a canopy of stars draped over the garden. They'd been working on it secretly, hoping to surprise Elspeth. Lyle had been in on the plan and he was sent into the knitting bee to distract the ladies while Brodrick arranged the champagne and special touches to the romantic setting. Brodrick had needed to switch the lights on to check that they were working as planned, but didn't want to alert Elspeth or the others at the knitting bee. And there had been an electrical glitch so he'd needed Lyle and Rory to help keep the ladies busy while he sorted it.

The knitting bee members, along with Lyle, Rory, Innis, Ean and Shuggie stood watching Brodrick get down on one knee and ask Elspeth to marry him.

'Will you marry me, Elspeth?' Brodrick's hopeful voice resonated in the cold, crisp air as he held up the jewellery box with a beautiful solitaire diamond ring set in white gold. The brilliant–cut of the large diamond represented the North Star, so bright and hopeful. It was something that had meant a lot to them as they'd fallen in love, admiring it in the clear night skies that were part of the island's beauty.

'Yes,' Elspeth said, smiling at Brodrick as he put the ring on her finger.

Her acceptance ignited a cheer from their friends. A special moment shared with the people they cared about.

Brodrick stood up and wrapped her in his arms and kissed her.

Beaming with excitement, Elspeth then looked round at all the smiling faces lit up in the warmth of the knitting bee.

Brodrick popped open the bottle of champagne and poured two glasses, tipped them in a loving cheers, and drank to their future happiness.

'Come in and join us for a celebratory drink,' Brodrick said, inviting them into the cafe bar. The premises was still open, and fairly busy with customers enjoying an evening meal, a drink and dancing. His staff had tended to customers while he'd set up his proposal.

Innis made a quick call to Finlay. 'Disaster averted. Brodrick proposed to Elspeth. She's accepted his ring. It looks like Lyle and Rory were in on his proposal plan and were creating a distraction while he set up a light display in his cafe bar's back garden.'

'So Rory stripping off his shirt was part of the plan?' said Finlay.

'No, I think their plan went awry and Rory had to cause a distraction,' Innis explained.

'A half–naked builder at the knitting bee,' Finlay said jokingly. 'Yes, that would work well.'

'We'll be back soon,' said Innis. 'And if you pop up to your turret, I'm sure you'll see Brodrick's garden lit up like a beacon.'

Finlay laughed as they ended the call.

The ladies decided to cut short their knitting bee and head next door to the cafe bar to celebrate the engagement. They walked through to the knitting shop and went in the front entrance of the cafe bar. Lyle and Rory went with them.

'I have to get back to my taxi,' said Shuggie. 'I'm kitten sitting Fluffy and someone wants picked up and driven to the castle.'

They waved Shuggie off.

Innis and Ean stood outside the cafe bar for a moment deciding what to do.

'We should go in for a wee while to celebrate with them,' said Ean. 'Then we can head back. The dinner dance was going well. Finlay can handle it.'

Innis agreed, then he saw a look on Ean's face as if something was troubling him.

The air wafting in from the sea was brisk. It was no night for standing chatting without being wrapped up warm.

'Is something wrong, Ean?'

Ean sighed heavily. 'Seeing Brodrick propose...it makes me want to ask Ailsa to marry me, but I know I need to wait until we've been dating a lot longer.' He shrugged and glanced out at the sea, feeling a longing to be settled. 'I'm ready to settle down. Do you know what I mean?'

'I do,' Innis admitted. 'It's tricky, finding the right balance, the right time to propose. I've seen you and Ailsa together. It's clear how much she loves you, and I've no doubts about your feelings for her. But I think you're right to wait, even until the New Year, like you've said you'd planned to do. Enjoy Christmas together. Ask her to the ball.'

Ean nodded. 'What about you? I see less of a lone wolf in you these days. But it's like you've got quicksilver in your veins, as if you're wanting to settle down, but can't settle within yourself because of Skye.'

Ean had nailed it. The elusive solution to the problem he had with his feelings for Skye, and not wanting to hurt her. Innis didn't say anything, but his silence confirmed that Ean was right.

'Whatever you're planning to do about you and Skye, or planning not to do, be careful. Don't risk losing her to someone else. Nothing is worth that.'

'When did you become so wise?' Innis said to his younger brother.

Ean laughed and shrugged off the compliment. 'You, me and Finlay. None of us have made a success of love and romance. Business, yes. Running the castle, definitely. You and your cake shop and

41

chocolatier work, yes. But the women in our lives...we've made some mistakes in the past. Let's try not to repeat them.'

'Has Finlay said anything to you recently about proposing to Merrilees?' said Innis.

'Only that he's thinking of asking her to marry him in the New Year.'

'Not at Christmastime?'

'No.'

'Why not? They're a strong match. Finlay thinks the world of her.'

Ean took a long breath. 'He says that this is the busiest time of the year at the castle. And it's the same for Merrilees and her work at the newspaper. Plus she's on a deadline to finish the romance novel she's been writing. He thinks there's too much happening and that the proposal would be lost in the melee of work and a crazy busy Christmas.'

Innis nodded thoughtfully.

'Are you two going to stand out here all night?' Brodrick called to them from the doorway of the cafe bar. 'Or are you coming in?'

Smiling, Innis and Ean headed inside, leaving the cold and their deep thoughts and romantic turmoil behind them.

Brodrick's cafe bar was classy, traditional, and decorated in rich, neutral tones that fitted perfectly with the modern world.

Shiny gold balustrades stretched along the edges of the bar, and mirrors behind it reflected the large bottles of whisky, brandy, gin, rum and other bottled spirits and liqueurs. A Christmas cocktail menu was pinned up beside the day's special menu board.

Vintage prints of the island were framed on the coffee and cream walls, and there was a small area for dancing on the dark wooden floor opposite the bar.

Dining tables were situated at the windows with a view of the main street and sea beyond, and around the main area, creating a welcoming cafe style ambiance for couples and larger parties. Brodrick had inherited money and invested it in the cafe bar. At first he lived above the premises, but as the profits accrued, he'd moved into a cottage up on the hills with a view of the sea. This would be the home he'd share with Elspeth when they were married. He couldn't wait. Now that she'd accepted his proposal, they aimed to make a date for their wedding, and planned to discuss this later in private.

The current menus catered for the festive season, but Brodrick had kept the ice cream counter open. The premises used to be a retro cafe selling ice cream, sticks of rock and souvenirs. Brodrick had modernised it when he'd bought it over, but kept the ice cream parlour element. Ice cream cones sold well in the summer and warmer months, but he'd found that the flavours ranging from chocolate and vanilla to mint and strawberry were equally popular in the winter. His Christmas cones were selling well, and along with the offer of a drink to celebrate his engagement, he enticed them to try his new festive flavours including a chocolate one as rich as the Yule log on the dinner menu.

'Help yourself to a glass of champagne,' Brodrick told Innis and Ean, gesturing to a tray on a table beside the bar. 'Or there's wine, beer or whisky if you prefer.'

Innis smiled and politely refused. 'I'm driving, but I wouldn't say no to a chocolate Christmas cone.'

Ean picked up a glass of champagne, while Brodrick scooped the ice cream into a cone and added chocolate sprinkles.

Music played in the background and mixed with the lively chatter, creating a buzz of excitement to the cafe bar. A gold tinsel Christmas tree sat near the entrance and was decorated with crystal clear twinkle lights.

Skye was waiting for one of the staff to make her a strawberry ice cream cone, while Ailsa enjoyed the delicious mint flavour.

'Come and have a pokey hat,' Ailsa called to Ean, encouraging him to have a cone.

Ean walked over to the pretty little ice cream parlour display to take her up on her suggestion. 'I'll have a butterscotch pokey hat.'

As they tucked into their cones, Ailsa smiled at him. 'How did the meeting go? Are you going to hold a ball at the castle?'

Ean called over to Innis who was standing talking to Brodrick having eaten his chocolate Christmas cone. 'Innis! Are we having a fairytale ball at the castle this Christmas Eve? Or not?' Ean's underlying smile encouraged Innis to speak up.

A lull descended over the company as Innis made the announcement. 'Yes, we are. So get your ball gowns and evening suits ready.'

Skye squealed, and not yet having been served with her cone, she ran over to Innis, jumped up and wrapped her arms around his neck, hugging him with joy.

Taken back for a second, Innis then savoured the moment, feeling this beautiful young woman full of love and laughter hug him until his heart ached for her.

'Someone is going to have to peel my sister off of Innis,' Holly said jokingly.

'I think Skye's pleased,' Ean said to Ailsa.

'We're all pleased,' Ailsa told him. 'If we weren't eating pokey hats, I'd be dangling around your neck too.'

Ean laughed. 'I'd better hurry up and finish this cone. I'm not missing out on that,' he teased her.

'Oh, sorry,' Skye apologised to Innis, unravelling herself from him and stepping back. 'Blame the champagne. But I'm just so happy that there's a ball this Christmas. I'll tell the suppliers to send the ball gowns, and I've other evening dresses in mind that would look gorgeous too.'

Innis gazed down at her, his heart still pounding from her loving embrace. 'It's fine. I'm happy you're happy.'

Smiling at him, her cheeks pink from blushing, Skye hurried away to join the other ladies.

Amid the laughter, the ladies buzzed around Elspeth, admiring her engagement ring and making wishes on it.

'It reminds me of the North Star,' Elspeth gushed. 'Brodrick said he bought it because it looked so brilliant and starlike.'

'Do I need to dust off my top hat and tails?' Brodrick said to Innis as they continued to chat. 'I've a dinner suit that I wore to a wedding reception.'

Innis grinned. 'Dress to impress. That's the code for the ball attire.'

'Can do.' Brodrick glanced over at Elspeth as she giggled and let the ladies try on her engagement ring. 'I'm sure my fiancée will look lovely in a ball gown.' Then he smiled. 'That's the first time I've said that. Fiancée has a nice ring to it.'

'It does indeed,' Innis agreed, realising how ardently he wished he could say the same for Skye. Noticing that the night was wearing on, he phoned Finlay.

'Still partying at the cafe bar?'

'Yes, so we're going to be a bit late. Ean's on the champagne and ice cream.'

'Sounds tasty,' said Finlay.

'It is. We should add more ice cream to our pudding menus.'

'I'll tell Nairne.'

Their head chef at the castle was Ailsa's uncle, Nairne, and although he had other chefs and catering staff to assist him, he was responsible for creating the menus for the guests when they were staying at the castle and for special functions.

The music in the background of the cafe bar notched up a gear into the lively zone.

'Have you been dancing with Skye?' There was a smile in Finlay's voice picturing Innis giving it large on the dance floor. Innis was skilled at the ceilidh dances and waltzes, but freestyle and gyrations wasn't his forte.

'No, but she hugged the breath from me when I announced that we're having a fairytale ball.'

Finlay laughed. 'Dance with her. Don't let her fun–loving attitude tonight go to waste.'

No reply from Innis.

'I take it there's talk of ball gowns and gladrags?' said Finlay.

'Galore. Skye told me she's telling the dress suppliers to send the ball gowns to their shop. And Brodrick is getting his top hat and tails out of the back of his wardrobe.'

'We'll need to up our game by the sounds of it. Bespoke ballroom wear for us? Or our dress kilts?'

'Decisions, decisions.'

'Tell Skye and Holly to keep a ball gown aside for me,' Merrilees shouted through to Innis. She was sitting at the private table with Finlay discussing their day's events, and overheard the conversation. 'And tell Elspeth and Brodrick congratulations on their engagement.'

'I'll do that,' Innis promised, feeling the momentum of the fairytale ball gather pace.

Finlay heard the excitement in Merrilees voice as she sent her congratulations to the happy couple. It made him wonder all the more if he should forgo his plan to ask her to marry him in the New Year and ask her now, at Christmastime, as Brodrick had done with Elspeth. Then again, he didn't want his proposal to seem like a knee–jerk reaction, following on from Brodrick asking Elspeth to be his wife. He wanted his

47

proposal to have its own merit and not become entwined with any other engagement.

'I'll start writing up the announcement for the ball to put on the website,' Finlay said to Innis. He glanced at Merrilees. 'Or perhaps our expert feature writer will use her journalist skills to write it for us.'

Merrilees laughed. 'I'm on it.' Then she gestured as if she was writing a news headline. 'Fairytale Christmas ball on the island.'

'We should advertise it in the press,' Finlay said, remembering how effective the previous feature had been, bringing more bookings and visitors to the castle.

'Yes, we should,' Innis agreed.

'I'm writing the entertainment features for the next issue of the paper,' said Merrilees. 'I could write your editorial tonight. Say, five hundred words. It would be on time for tomorrow night's deadline.'

'Do that,' Finlay confirmed.

'I'll message my editor. He'll talk to the advertising manager. We can make this happen,' Merrilees promised, used to the fast pace of her newspaper work in Glasgow.

'We don't have the details.' Innis sounded concerned. 'Do you want me to come up with some ideas?'

'It's okay,' Merrilees assured him. 'I'll waffle on about the magnificent castle on the Scottish island. Snow guaranteed in time for the ball on Christmas Eve. A delicious buffet and dancing under chandeliers in a ballroom size function suite, with a huge Christmas tree sparkling with fairy lights.'

'I'm sold. Book me two tickets,' Finlay joked. 'You coming with me, Merrilees?'

'Oh, yes. I'm excited about buying a ball gown.'

With their plans set, they finished the call, and Merrilees started making notes for the news feature.

CHAPTER FOUR

The impromptu engagement party notched up a gear at the cafe bar. The knitting bee members were happily dancing the night away — and this included the makeshift members, Lyle and Rory.

Brodrick had danced mainly with Elspeth, but they'd become separated as the knitting bee ladies buzzed around her again. He stepped back to let them fuss over her, and took a breather at the side of the bar where Innis was standing watching Skye and Holly dancing with Lyle while Rory bopped around with Rowen.

'Not making a move to ask Skye to dance with you?' Brodrick said to Innis.

Innis shrugged his broad shoulders. He wasn't sure if he would. He wasn't certain he wouldn't.

Changing the conversation to the subject of business, Brodrick brought up Innis' recent trip to the mainland. 'How is your chocolatier work fairing? Did your business trip go okay?'

'It did. Very worthwhile. I was looking for specialist chocolate to use for my new range of confectionary.'

'The new festive chocolates that I've seen in your cake shop window?'

'Yes, but beyond that. As I'm sure you know, we both live months, sometimes seasons ahead, planning menus and events for our businesses.'

'It's a full–time task. Thankfully, we both love our work. I'm already planning menus for the New Year.'

Innis had a thought. 'I brought back a load of different flavours and types of chocolate samples. Too many for me to use. Would you like some to try out new recipes for your ice cream? I don't make chocolate, as I'm always having to tell folk. I use top quality chocolate to make my chocolatier confectionary. The selection of chocolate I brought back from the cities is excellent.'

Brodrick was pleasantly taken aback. 'Yes, I'll pay you for them.'

'Away and chase yourself,' Innis told him with a grin. 'I'll bring the samples down tomorrow. I've been working on new recipes in the castle kitchen and storing the chocolate there. The kitchen is huge, one of those old–fashioned kitchens where there are larders for storing and cooling everything. The chocolate keeps better up there than at the cake shop where the ovens create quite a bit of heat in the wee kitchen. I'm planning to extend the premises into the garden at the back of the cake shop.'

'You mentioned that a while ago.'

'I put my plans on hold because I thought Morven was going to retire early and sell the knitting shop,' Innis admitted. 'Obviously I'm happy that Elspeth moved in with her aunt and the island still has the knitting shop which is better for everyone. So now I'm thinking of hiring Murdo and Rory to do the building work on the cake shop extension.'

Brodrick laughed. 'Rory?'

'I know,' Innis agreed, 'but he's a top notch builder. Have you seen what he's done with the old house in the middle of nowhere? He bought it for a song.'

'No, but I've heard the gossip that it's a complete transformation into a first–class mansion,' said Brodrick.

'I drove by recently. It's like a new building. I like the architecture that Rory's added. He's got talent.'

'My ears are burning,' a voice said behind them.

They looked round to see Rory walking over to the bar, grinning at them.

'What is it they say about eavesdropping...?' Brodrick joked with Rory.

Innis came right out with his plan. 'I'd like to hire you to do the work, along with Murdo.'

'Murdo and me work well together. Look what we did with the stage and the runway for the fashion show,' said Rory.

'Exactly,' Innis told him. 'So what do you say?'

'I say yes. When do you want me to start drawing up sketches?'

'Sooner rather than later, unless you're busy with work just now,' said Innis.

'I'll pop round tomorrow and take a few measurements, get the ball rolling.' Rory extended his hand to Innis.

They shook hands firmly.

'Rory! Come and dance with me,' Rowen called over to him.

Happy to accommodate his girlfriend, Rory went over to join her.

Brodrick decided to pluck Elspeth from the midst of the chatter and dance with her again.

Ean was up dancing with Ailsa.

Innis stood on his own watching Skye now dancing with another local man who looked delighted to be in her company.

Come on, Innis urged himself. Don't be a fool again.

When Skye and Holly took a breather from the dancing, Innis walked over to them.

'Merrilees asked me to tell you to keep a ball gown aside for her,' Innis said to them, using this as an excuse to go over and chat.

'We will,' Holly assured him.

'I saw a couple of ball gowns listed that would suit Merrilees.' Skye beamed a smile at Innis.

Lyle wandered over to them. 'Would you care to dance with me?' he said to Holly.

'Okay,' Holly said brightly, and walked away with Lyle.

Innis had two choices. Three if he was being an idiot. Continue chatting to Skye. Walk away having passed on Merrilees' message. Or ask Skye to dance.

Skye closed down all three options with one comment. 'I love this song.' Her words hung in the air along with her anticipation that he'd dance with her.

Innis was pleased to take the hint. The song was reasonably lively, and they danced separately, moving to the upbeat tune, but then it faded and merged with a slow, romantic number, leaving Innis and Skye standing there separately for a lingering moment.

Taking charge of the situation, Innis held out his hand to Skye. 'Shall we?'

Skye accepted his invitation for a slow waltz that was the closing dance of the night. The party had been impromptu, but social nights at the cafe bar could be as fun as any large function. Often it all came down to the last dance of the night. And here they were dancing close together to a song that spoke of love and romance.

Holding Skye in his arms, he felt her softness and her strength. The woman who made him smile more than anyone ever had. Her forthright attitude and fun–loving nature was the perfect blend for him. But was he the right man for her? Would his strength diminish hers? Would his serious character dim the brightness that radiated from her? Or would they balance each other in ways that would make him become a better man?

Before he could dwell further, while feeling her move so close to him, she leaned back and smiled up at him to reveal a secret.

'When I was cycling back along the main street from the post office earlier, the stars were starting to appear in the sky. The North Star, the brightest, shone so clearly that I made a wish upon it.'

'A wish? Is it a secret? Or can't you tell in case that makes it not come true?'

'It did come true.' Her smile lit up her beautiful blue eyes. 'I wished that there would be a fairytale ball at the castle this Christmas.'

His smile poured from the depths of his heart. 'I'm glad your wish came true.'

She leaned into him again as he held her in hold, one hand in his, the other on his broad shoulder, her head leaning close to his.

'Do you think you'll make another wish on the North Star?' he whispered to her.

'No, I don't want to push my luck. But maybe you should try, unless you've used up all your wishes.'

He hadn't used one. But perhaps it was time he tried.

Without another word, they danced together until the music ended.

Everyone filtered outside the cafe bar into the night, all heading home in different directions. Shuggie's taxi was ready and waiting to drop a number of them off at their cottages. Others lived up on the nearby hills and walked home having had a great night.

Innis gazed out at the vast sky across the sea. Light reflected through the darkness, creating a pink hue. The sky above the island, so clear that it showed so many stars, had a glow to it even in the evenings as the light bounded off the sea all along the coast, stretching far into the distant islands.

'Snow is on its way,' Innis said almost to himself, but others heard his voice in the quiet night.

His amber eyes recognised that familiar pink tint that brought the snow with it. Usually he saw it from the top of the hills on the evenings he stood there on his own admiring the view of the island. Since he was a boy, he'd seen this. And he could sense it too. There was a sense of snow in the air. Not tonight, not tomorrow, but perhaps tomorrow evening around twilight.

'Nah!' Rory said, standing hands on hips and looking out at the sea. 'The snow isn't forecast until next week. I keep a check on the weather because of my building work. It's probably going to rain a wee bit though. A rainy day tomorrow.'

Innis disagreed, but was not in the mood to argue vehemently. 'The snow's coming soon.' He walked over to his car. 'Anyone wanting a lift home?'

'Come on, Ailsa,' Ean beckoned to her. 'We'll drop you off.'

'It's fine. I'm walking home with Skye and Holly,' said Ailsa.

'Pile in,' Innis told them, turning on the engine to create some heat in the car.

Ean opened the rear door to Innis' expensive car.

Ailsa, Skye and Holly sat together in the back seat while Ean sat up front.

'Thanks for a great night,' Innis called to Brodrick as he stood outside the cafe bar with his arm around Elspeth's shoulder as he waved everyone off. 'And congratulations again on your engagement. I'll pop down in the morning with the chocolate,' he reminded him, and then drove off up the hill to take the ladies home to their respective houses.

Elspeth frowned at Brodrick. 'Chocolate?'

'Come on, it's cold out here. I'll explain inside.' Brodrick swept his fiancée into the cafe bar, hoping to discuss their wedding plans before calling it a night.

Innis parked outside Ailsa's cottage first. She'd inherited the lovely cottage when her grandmother left to move to the mainland. Ailsa used the cottage for her craft work, along with owning her own shop in the main street. Winter flowers grew around the door and it was decorated with fairy lights.

Ean stepped out and walked Ailsa to the front door, saw that she got in safe, kissed her goodnight and then went back to the car.

Innis then drove the short distance to drop off Skye and Holly at their parents' house. Their parents were away a lot, visiting family and friends in the nearby islands and on the mainland since their mother retired and handed the dress shop to them.

Innis kept the engine running and they waited until Skye and Holly opened their door and waved them off before driving down the hill and along the coast road.

Ean looked out at the sea and the sky. 'Do you really think it's going to snow a bit earlier this year?'

'I do.' There was no hesitation.

'Once the snow comes, it'll be a whiteout until well after the New Year.'

'It will, but the perfect setting for a fairytale ball.' Innis shot a glance at Ean.

'We've got a load of planning to do. But I don't mind. I'm looking forward to it, and so is Ailsa.' He paused and then commented, 'You and Skye were looking cosy close dancing tonight.'

Ean's comment hung in the air for a moment.

Innis drove away from the coast into the road leading to the forest and the castle's estate.

'Did you ask Skye to go to the ball with you?' Ean prompted him.

'No. Maybe I will. She's advised me to make a wish on the North Star. Hers apparently came true. We're having a ball.'

Ean laughed. 'A wish on the North Star.'

Innis pressed his firm lips together and nodded.

Ean peered out the window, craning to see if he could find it in among the myriad of stars in the sky. Halfway up the forest road, he thought he saw it. 'Pull the car over. I want to view the stars.'

Innis pull over on the quiet road. Not another car went by.

Ean stepped outside, breathing in the scent of the pine trees and greenery that overtook the sea air. He gazed up. 'There it is.' He pointed directly up to it.

His curiosity sparked, Innis got out and looked up at the brightest star shining in the sky.

'I'm making a wish,' said Ean, hinting that he wanted a moment to concentrate.

Innis let him get on with it without interruption, though he'd no intention of making one too.

'Okay. I hope it comes true. Obviously, I can't tell you what it was or it won't come true. I know it's a long shot that it will. But if I don't try...' He shrugged, and then looked at Innis. 'Your turn.'

Innis shook his head and walked back to the car.

'Come on. You've nothing to lose,' Ean reasoned.

Innis stood beside the car. The star was still glittering above him. 'What if what I wish for isn't right for Skye?'

'Then you're not wishing for the right thing,' Ean advised. 'Adjust your wish to make it right.'

58

Innis' lips formed a wry smile. 'Whatever happened to my wee brother? Now he's full of great advice.'

'We both grew up. Both older. Neither of us wiser, but I'm trying not to throw barriers in my own way. You should too. Come on, it's freezing out here. Make a wish. The knitting bee ladies were all making wishes on Elspeth's engagement ring. And Skye's wish came true about the ball. Maybe it's a great night for making wishes.'

'I'm not really into wishes and fairytales.'

Ean blinked at him and gestured around him. 'We live in a fairytale castle on one of the most beautiful islands imaginable. We're standing in a fantastic forest near thistle loch and a waterfall that's all lit up at night. And we're planning a ball for Christmas Eve.'

Innis nodded and smiled. Then he gazed up at the North Star. He took a moment to think what his wish would be — and then hoped with all his heart.

'Yes!' Ean said, punching the air.

'Can we go home now?' Innis got into the car.

'To our fairytale castle?' Ean joked with him.

'Don't push it,' Innis warned him playfully. 'And don't tell anyone what I just did.'

'My lips are sealed,' Ean promised, gesturing that he'd zipped them shut and threw the key away.

Innis laughed, and drove them on through the forest towards the castle.

The dark stone grandeur of the castle emerged as they drove towards the entrance. Lights glowed from the windows, and the dinner dance was still in full flow. The overarching trees above the ornate gates that were wide open led through the gardens to the castle.

As they drove in, Merrilees drove out.

She waved to them from her car as she headed away from the castle to the cottage she was living in. During her trips to the mainland for her photo–journalism work, she left her car at the castle. Her schedule was flexible, but she tended to work at the newspaper office in Glasgow one day a week, and email her editorials to her editor the remainder of the time.

Innis and Ean waved to her, familiar with her routine. After arriving back from Glasgow on the ferry, she'd take a taxi to the castle to spend time with Finlay even though he was tending to the functions and parties most nights. Instead of moving in with Finlay to his suite of rooms in the castle, she'd accepted his offer to stay in one of the holiday cottages that was part of the castle's estate. This enabled her to retain her independence and a place of her own where she could work on her romance novel, and her journalistic work for the newspaper in Glasgow. The best of both worlds, especially for a writer who needed time on her own to work and be creative.

Finlay took the cottage off the estate's holiday listing on the castle's website. The lease was given to Merrilees until well into the New Year. Finlay had handed her the key. It was a safe and secure place to live.

The cottage was one she was familiar with having been brought up on the island. As a young girl, she'd loved stargazer cottage and its garden, that she imagined was magical. It certainly looked magical during the summer days when she'd watch the bees, butterflies and dragonflies flit through the flowers in the garden that merged with the forest.

Murdo had recently given the pretty cottage a fresh overhaul, and had tended and tamed the garden.

But it was the view that made it extra special. A skylight window in the bedroom offered a fantastic view of the stars.

Merrilees parked her car outside the cottage, grabbed her bag that was loaded with work, and walked through the garden to the front door. A spare key was kept under an ornamental owl beside the flower pots, and she retrieved the key and unlocked the door.

The outside was picturesque, but the inside was equally impressive.

The living room's light cream decor had touches of pastel blue and white, and a chintz couch and chairs provided a cosy niche to come home to.

She shrugged her bag from her shoulder along with the weight of the hectic day and lit the fire.

The decor throughout the cottage was fresh and clean with a cosiness from the fire and the pretty lamps. And her Christmas tree was aglow with fairy lights.

Putting the kettle on to make tea, she went through to the bedroom to change into her comfy pyjamas and slippers.

The large skylight above the double bed had a view of the stars in the night sky.

Stargazer cottage was the perfect bolthole for her to write her novel. The deadline was looming, but she was within a chapter of finishing it ready to send it off to her publishers.

But first, she planned to write the news feature for the castle's ball and email it to her editor. So that's what she did.

Sitting by the fireside, sipping her tea, she set up her laptop and wrote an enticing editorial about the castle's fairytale ball. She was used to working to tight deadlines, so she finished it and sent it off to the newspaper editor.

Then she continued writing her novel until late in the night. She wasn't heading to the mainland in the morning. No early start, no hustle and bustle of the newspaper, so she worked until she'd finished the next part of the story.

Finally, she closed her laptop, and with the fire barely aglow now, she went to bed.

Lying there, she gazed up at the stars through the skylight. The North Star was clear to see, and since living in the cottage she'd taken an interest in stargazing and tried to learn the main constellations. She loved the starry skies on the island.

Blinking, she thought she saw a couple of snowflakes drift by the skylight, but they were gone when she looked again. She chalked it up to tiredness and settled down, pulling the quilt up around her. Snow wasn't forecast until next week. Yes, she thought, drifting off to sleep, the snowflakes were just her imagination. Part of the wonder of living in a fairytale cottage.

CHAPTER FIVE

Innis and Ean joined Finlay in the castle's function room as the dinner dance came to a close. They sat at their private table discussing the night's events.

'I thought we could start planning the ball in the morning,' Finlay suggested. 'Merrilees let me see the rough editorial she's writing for the advertising feature in the newspaper. I trust her to write something great. It's ideal because it doesn't go into details of the buffet menu or anything like that. It just highlights that we're holding a ball at the castle on Christmas Eve.'

'That's what we need at the moment,' Ean agreed.

'Once we have details of the menu and other aspects, we can add those as news to our website,' said Finlay.

They all agreed.

'We were impressed with Brodrick's range of ice cream tonight,' said Innis. 'I think we should include more ice cream on our menus.'

'Brodrick says it sells well in the winter,' Ean confirmed.

Finlay nodded. 'Yes, we should.'

Innis stood up. 'I told Brodrick I'd give him some chocolate samples to try out new flavours for his ice cream,' Innis told Finlay. 'I'm going through to the kitchen to wrap them up. I'll mention to Nairne about adding ice cream to the menus.'

'Do that,' said Finlay. 'And tell him we'll have a meeting tomorrow after breakfast to discuss the buffet for the ball.'

'I'll tell him,' Innis confirmed.

Nairne was finishing up in the kitchen when Innis walked in.

The castle kitchen was so large that it easily accommodated Innis' chocolatier set up. Shelves were stacked with boxes ready to be filled with chocolates. Cupboards stored all the products he used to create everything from chocolate truffles to fondant fancies in dark, milk and white chocolate.

The facility had a butler sink, ovens, and worktop where Innis could mix his specialist confectionary.

The back door opened out on to the patio where Innis and his brothers liked to have breakfast most mornings unless it was lashing rain.

Everything in the chocolatier part of the kitchen gleamed under the lights, and the aroma of chocolate wafted through the air as Innis started packing the samples to give to Brodrick.

'We're thinking of adding ice cream to the castle menus,' Innis said to Nairne.

'Great. Whenever there's ice cream on the pudding menu, it's always the first thing to go.'

'What flavours are popular?'

Nairne reached for one of the recipe books on the shelf where he'd tucked in lists that he used when preparing ideas for the menus. 'According to my notes, vanilla and chocolate, then mint and strawberry. Obviously, we added our own touches but the traditional flavours are the most popular, but I'd like to include others like the butterscotch that Brodrick sells in his cafe bar.'

'Ean had that tonight, in a cone. I tried the chocolate Christmas ice cream. It was delicious.' He gestured to the samples he was packing up and putting into a large cake box. 'I'm giving Brodrick samples of the chocolate I brought back recently to let him try new recipes.'

'Are we going to include ice cream on the buffet menu for the ball? We've got the chilled counter that we use during the summer for the sorbet and ice cream.'

'Yes, I think we should. Finlay is planning a meeting to discuss this with you tomorrow.'

'We could buy the ice cream from Brodrick, offer a selection of the flavours he's got, including the chocolate Christmas one and butterscotch.'

Innis nodded firmly. 'I'll talk to Brodrick about this in the morning when I give him the chocolate samples.'

Nairne smiled. 'Great. And you should talk to Lyle too. He has catered for big fancy balls when he was training as a patisserie chef. He has a lot of experience.'

Innis frowned. 'Lyle?'

'Yes, don't underestimate his skills. He's made a success of his tea shop due to the delicious cakes and bakery items he makes. Many of them are his own recipes.'

Innis thought about how Lyle had opened the tea shop after training as a patisserie chef on the mainland. And now he'd recently expanded the premises to the upstairs level, creating a modern vintage style of tea shop.

'I'll pop in to the tea shop and have a word with Lyle too.'

'Lyle could provide us with extra cakes for the ball,' Nairne suggested.

Innis agreed.

Leaving Innis to get on with his packing, Nairne left to go home.

'I'll see you in the morning,' Nairne said, giving a cheery wave.

Innis continued packing and then worked on until late, trying out a new recipe he had in mind for his chocolates. He liked mixing flavours and textures.

The night wore on and he tidied up and switched the lights off.

The night porter at the reception desk bid him goodnight as Innis headed upstairs to get some sleep.

But sleep didn't come easy as his mind replayed dancing with Skye, feeling her in his arms, her softness, her beauty...

Punching his pillows into comfy submission, he forced himself to settle down before the dawn when he'd be up early to start another busy day.

Skye had snuggled down to sleep, but her dreams were filled with Innis. She blamed the moments of closeness they'd shared at the cafe bar. The way he held her when they danced. Those intense amber eyes gazing down at her. Tempting her? She wasn't sure. Maybe the attraction she felt for him was causing her imagination to fill in the gaps of all the things he didn't say. At least not verbally. Though the unspoken

Brodrick came over and lifted the lids. 'That's a lot more than I anticipated. Are you sure you can spare this?'

Innis nodded firmly. 'I brought back far more than I needed, mainly so I could try out all the different types from the various suppliers. I've plenty.'

'Thanks very much.' Brodrick was sincere. 'White chocolate? That looks wonderful.'

'It is. And so is the milk and variations of the dark blends.'

'I'll be experimenting with all of these.' The enthusiasm sounded in Brodrick's voice.

'There was something I wanted to talk to you about. We're planning to have ice cream as part of the buffet menu for the ball. Would you be able to supply us with it?'

Brodrick brightened at the thought of such an order. 'I could. How much to you estimate you'll need? And what flavours do you want?'

'We've still to meet and chat with Nairne about this. But if you're interested, we'll be able to tell you by the end of the day. What I do know is...we want all the flavours.'

Brodrick smiled. 'I can do that. Would that include the Christmas flavour?'

'Especially that one. It tasted delicious and it's ideal for our Christmas Eve theme.'

'Okay. I'll put my mind to it.'

'Right, I'm popping in to talk to Lyle now.'

'He's catered for prestigious balls at fancy events in the past.'

'So I've heard. I know his bakery products are popular with customers, but I'd no idea he was such an experienced patisserie chef.'

Brodrick lowered his tone. 'I think we underestimate him because...well, Lyle is Lyle.'

Innis smiled and nodded, then headed out and along to the nearby tea shop.

Lyle was cooking in the kitchen, but he'd already stacked up cakes in the display cabinets, everything filled ready for the customers coming for their daily baking orders.

Innis followed the tasty aroma through to the kitchen. Something savoury was cooking along with the scent of cakes and scones baking. 'Morning.'

Lyle jolted and then smiled. 'Oh, it's yourself.' Innis' casual manner indicated that nothing was awry, but Lyle was surprised to see him.

'I can see you're busy baking, but can I talk to you while you work?'

'Yes, come on in. There's a fresh pot of tea. Help yourself to a cuppa. And there's sausage rolls warm from the oven if you want one.' Lyle wore his chef's whites and was mixing a bowl of buttercream.

'I've had breakfast...but they do smell tasty.'

'Ach, take one. It'll put strength in your stride for the busy day ahead.'

Innis didn't need to be offered this twice. He helped himself to a cup of tea and a sausage roll. Biting into the light puff pastry and savoury filling, he nodded and gave Lyle the thumbs up.

Lyle laughed. 'Don't fuss about the crumbs and flakes. Tuck in.' He added vanilla to the buttercream and kept working. 'So...can I guess why you're here?'

Innis nodded and continued to eat the sausage roll.

'Do you need extra cakes for the ball? Do you want me to bake some?'

Innis sipped his tea and then explained. 'Yes and something else.'

Lyle frowned while he whipped the buttercream for the cupcakes and Victoria sponges.

'Advice,' Innis told him. 'Nairne says you've catered for balls like the one we're having.'

'That's true. It was part of my training. What is it you need to know?'

'We're having a buffet as that's always what works when we have a large dinner dance. With couples up dancing at the ball, we want to clear the main floor area so they can waltz around, so a buffet along the far side wall works well.'

'The balls I worked on did the same. I think there's a main difference between a dinner dance and a ball. The first often has people that attend for the dinner, but say they're not there for the dancing. But if you go to a ball, you go there to dance. You dress to impress and to enjoy dancing, and that's the core of what a ball is. Anything else is just a fancy dinner dance.'

Innis nodded, taking in this advice. 'That's a very relevant point.'

'And one to highlight when you're advertising your fairytale ball. It'll raise the bar on the whole event.'

'We'll do that.'

Lyle reached up to a shelf of books and selected one. 'Take this with you. There are recipes for large buffets, for weddings and such, other recipes I used are tucked inside, and scribbled notes I made. It'll give you and the others ideas for the buffet menu.'

'Thanks, Lyle. I appreciate it. I'll bring it back to you soon. And thanks for the tea and sausage roll.'

A timer pinged on one of the ovens and Lyle lifted out a batch of scones. These were popular served plain to customers or split and filled with whipped cream and strawberry or raspberry jam.

Smiling, Lyle waved him off.

Walking through to the front of the tea shop on his way out, Innis viewed the cakes and bakery items on display in the glass cabinets with a fresh eye. The selection was impressive. All the cakes were beautifully made, from the traditional Victoria sponges filled with buttercream and jam and sprinkled with icing sugar or white icing and a cherry, to the festive fruit cakes bursting with sultanas and raisins and decorated with almonds and a shiny sugar glaze. Some had a dash of whisky. He could see the expertise, the talent that Lyle had. The scones were light and fluffy with a hint of golden brown. Often the hardest things to bake were the basics. But Lyle did it all to perfection. No wonder his tea shop was so successful.

Innis didn't grudge Lyle his success. Their shops were different and complemented each other, as did Brodrick's cafe bar, all catering to various tastes.

The fire was lit and the tea shop had retained the old–fashioned tiled fireplace where two tables were situated. Other tables were placed around the shop and seating was now available upstairs too. But customers could come in a buy what they wanted from Lyle as if it was a bakery shop.

On his way out, the morning breeze blew in from the sea, and there was that scent of snow again. Maybe the first fall would be later tonight. He planned to take a walk up the hills after closing for the day before going home to the castle.

And then he saw Skye and Holly drive up carrying armfuls of parcels they'd collected from the early delivery at the post office.

Skye glanced round, sensing she was being watched, or sensing Innis... She smiled at him.

He smiled back at her, his heart reacting to seeing her again. There were decisions to make regarding romance as well as business. But this morning, business took the lead. Unlocking his door, he went into the cake shop and started to get the day organised, beginning with heating the ovens, washing his hands, putting on his chef's clean clothing, and making a start on the cakes.

He put Lyle's recipe book safely away in a cupboard, intending to read it later, but he called Finlay to update him on the things he'd discussed with Brodrick and Lyle.

'Murdo's down at the post office collecting the mail and the daily papers for the guests. I'll ask him to pop in and get the book from you. Ean and I can use it to show Nairne when we're planning the buffet menu later this morning.'

'I'll have it ready for him. But thankfully, they're both up for helping with the ball. We'll discuss payment with them of course later.'

'Yes,' said Finlay.

They ended the call on a busy note, planning to keep in touch as they whittled down the buffet menu selection while Innis worked in his cake shop.

Innis put the book in a paper bag so that none of the notes were lost, ready for Murdo to pick up.

He went through to check the cakes on display and put the main lights on ready for Rosabel and Primrose arriving to help with the shop. From the window he saw Skye and Holly unloading delivery boxes from their car. Filled with dresses probably...

'I'm so excited.' Skye carried the last of the boxes into their vintage dress shop. She put it down with the others, several large boxes. 'I love when we get a job lot delivery of dresses. It's like opening presents on Christmas morning.'

Skye started to tear open the top of one of them.

'Did you even check roughly what you were buying when you ordered them?' Holly kept her fingers crossed that the dresses were as lovely as the tea dresses they'd bought the previous week.

'No. The message came through from them asking if we'd like to buy a job lot of vintage evening dresses. It was a real bargain. I clicked the order button and here we are. They're a regular supplier and they've never done us wrong.'

Holly nodded. 'Okay. What pressie are we opening first?'

'This one.' Skye pried it open, seeing a hint of pale blue satin peeking out. Opening it further, she lifted out a sky blue satin evening dress with shoestring straps decorated with matching sequins. 'This is lovely.' She draped it on a hanger and hung it up on a rail.

Holly pulled out the next dress, a confection of chiffon in cream shot through with gold thread. 'This is a contender for the ball gown collection.' She added it to the rail.

'Oh look at this.' Skye opened another box and pulled out a dress with an emerald velvet bodice that flowed down to a full–length tulle skirt that was a few shades lighter than the emerald.

Holly took charge of the dress. 'I do like this one.'

Dress after dress they unpacked each design, estimating the eras ranging from decades past.

Once the dresses were hanging on the rail and the boxes tidied away, they started to examine each dress for wear and tear. Every dress they sold was carefully cleaned, mended when necessary, embellished if it enhanced the design, and then sold in the shop and from their online store. Online sales dominated, but with the party season upon them, more local customers were coming in to browse and buy.

They expected an influx of customers wanting a ball gown and these were due to arrive within the next two days. But Skye had been tempted by the bargain offer of a job lot of evening dresses from a supplier on the mainland, and the contents of the boxes had not disappointed.

'Every one of these dresses is a winner,' said Holly. 'You were right to order the job lot.'

Skye smiled. 'These look like they've been worn once, maybe to a party or dance, and then hung in the wardrobe never to be worn again.'

'Classy designs. From about the forties and fifties I'd say by the looks of the stitching and finish.'

Skye agreed with Holly. 'I'll add new sequins to the blue dress. A few are missing from the straps. And I'll probably add a scattering of them on the bodice to highlight the design.'

Skye and Holly were both experienced in dressmaking, mending and upgrading dresses from bygone times. Skye's pink sewing machine was permanently set up behind the counter, and repairs were part of the fun of their work. They loved vintage fashion, especially dresses like these where the luxury of silks, satins, chiffons, tulle and velvet combined to create exquisite pieces that their customers clambered for.

In a corner of the shop was a bargain rail filled with summer dresses in light cotton and linen fabrics. Customers often picked up a bargain from out of season dresses. But Skye and Holly had gained a reputation for selling authentic vintage dresses, real bargains, throughout the year.

They'd acquired an extensive list of suppliers on the mainland, many in the cities like Glasgow, Edinburgh and London, from their mother. Over the years she'd owned the shop, she'd build up a reliable list of suppliers and they were happy to now deal with Skye and Holly. With the ferry making daily deliveries

76

to the island, orders could be sent easily back and forth. Since taking over their mother's shop, they'd increased sales substantially through their hard work, fashion work experience and love of all things in vintage clothing.

Holly pulled down a roll of light blue chiffon from the selection of fabrics they kept in their shop. She held it beside the blue silk dress. 'It's a fair match. We could add a full chiffon skirt to create a ball gown.'

'That would look wonderful.' Skye then lifted other chiffon, tulle and organza fabric from the shelves and held them up against the various dresses. The chiffon was soft and flowing and had a beautiful drape to it, while the organza had a more structured quality to it. 'Most of these dresses could be transformed into designs fit for the ball. And there's time to order other fabric. I saw some lovely chiffon, organza and georgette fabric that had lots of sparkle in it.'

'Let's do it,' Holly agreed, feeling the excitement build.

After sorting everything, Skye picked up her purse. 'I don't know about you, but I'm hungry.' They'd both skipped breakfast to make an early start. 'Would you like something from Lyle's tea shop?'

'Yes, anything delicious.'

'That doesn't exactly narrow it down. You know what Lyle's shop's like. Everything is delicious.'

'That should make it extra easy.'

Skye smiled and was about to leave when Ailsa came bursting in.

'What do you think?' Ailsa wore a glittering tiara–style hair band and turned her head back and forth to show how it sparkled under the lights.

'Very sparkly. Very you,' said Holly.

'Did you make it?' Skye admired the band on her friend's dark, silky hair.

Ailsa owned the craft shop nearby. She sold items that she made, and some she didn't. Her artistic skills were well known especially when it came to jewellery making and accessories.

'Yes, months ago,' said Ailsa. 'I was sorting through my stock and found it where I'd stashed it along with another four.'

'You have more than one?' Skye's interest perked up.

'Uh–huh!' She took the band off and handed it to Skye. 'Try it on. The others are all variations of sparkle from crystal to silver and gold — and pink.' Ailsa smiled knowingly as she emphasised the latter.

'Pink?' Skye paused from trying on the band.

'You mentioned last night that you had your eye on a pale pink ball gown. The pink hair band would look lovely with your dress.'

Skye put the band on and admired it in the shop's dressing room mirror. 'It looks like a tiara.'

'Without actually being a tiara,' said Ailsa. 'It's not like the ball is a fancy dress party. But these are just hair bands that happen to look like tiaras. Not too ostentatious.'

'No, not at all,' Skye agreed, reluctant to take it off.

'Let me try it on,' said Holly, eager to see if she'd suit it.

'The colour of the gold sparkles really enhances your auburn hair,' Ailsa told Holly.

'It does,' Skye confirmed. 'Obviously it would depend on your ball gown, but the gold would go with most dress colours.'

'I'll buy it,' Holly said firmly.

'Don't be silly. I made these for buttons and for fun. Keep it. And you can have the pink one.' She'd brought it with her in her bag.

Skye laughed. 'You know me too well.'

'That's what friends are for. Now did I hear you say that you were popping to the tea shop?' said Ailsa. 'I'm going there for something tasty for my morning tea.'

'I'll go with you.'

Leaving Holly in the shop, still wearing the tiara hair band, they walked to the tea shop.

Lyle saw them through the window. They often turned up to buy scones and cakes, but this morning they paused outside and seemed to be whispering and giggling in a conspiratorial way. They were up to something.

'Morning, Lyle,' Skye chirped as they walked up to the main counter.

'What can I get for you ladies today?' He gestured to the fruit scones and fairy cakes, knowing their tastes.

'I'd like a roll with Scottish cheddar and salad,' said Ailsa, in the mood for something savoury rather than sweet.

'That sounds tasty. Make that three. Holly and I have a delivery of gorgeous dresses to sort so this will combine as breakfast and lunch.'

Lyle made up their orders.

'And I'll have two fruit scones with strawberry jam,' Skye added.

As they paid for their orders, Skye spoke up. 'Does Rory take bookings for parties?' she said to Lyle.

Lyle frowned, unsure what she meant.

'And does he dance?' Ailsa wanted to know.

Lyle was flummoxed. 'Dance?'

'You know, sexy dancing,' Ailsa told him.

This confused Lyle even more. 'I don't know what you're talking about.'

'There's a picture of Rory pinned up on the notice board in the post office,' Skye explained. 'People can add their names if they want to hire him for parties.'

'Parties? What do you mean?' Lyle sounded anxious.

'You know how Rory stripped his shirt off last night at the knitting bee, showing us his lean muscles,' said Skye. 'Well, people are looking to hire him and want to know if he does any extras, like dancing or singing while he takes his clothes off.'

The tone of Skye's voice and Ailsa's innocent expression threw Lyle for a loop. 'Look after the tea shop for me. I'll be back in a few minutes.' He rushed towards the front door when Skye called after him.

'We were just joking.'

Lyle came to a sudden halt, turned and faced them, trying and failing not to laugh. 'You wee minxes! You had me fooled there. I knew the pair of you were up to something when I saw you whispering outside the shop.'

'Sorry, Lyle,' Ailsa apologised. 'We couldn't resist.'

Lyle walked back to the counter, shaking his head at them.

Holding up her bag of rolls and scones, Skye giggled and waved, leaving Lyle to point a warning finger at them.

'There will be payback for your mischief,' he said.

'No, don't ration our scones and cakes.' Skye feigned distress.

Lyle laughed, feeling lighter having had the two troublemakers in his tea shop.

CHAPTER SIX

Rory saw Skye and Ailsa hurrying out of the tea shop giggling and laughing. He'd parked his white van outside the cake shop ready to go in to discuss the extension work with Innis. But intrigued, he went into the tea shop first.

'What's going on with Skye and Ailsa?' Rory thumbed behind him as he strode up to Lyle at the counter.

Lyle was refilling his scone display and still in a playful mood. 'There's a poster of you up in the post office. People think you do strip dancing for parties and want to book you for Christmas.'

Rory gasped. 'Is this because I took my shirt off at the knitting bee last night?'

Lyle nodded, pressing his lips together to stifle his laughter.

Rory ran an anxious hand through the front of his thick blond hair. 'There's no way I'm dancing for folk at parties and taking my duds off. I'm going to take that poster down!' Rory rushed for the door.

'I was just kidding,' Lyle shouted after him.

Rory skidded to a halt and spun around, glaring at Lyle. His pale blue eyes lit up with fire. 'Why you cheeky—'

Two customers came in, unaware of what was happening. The ladies headed for the cake display to select cream doughnuts and chocolate eclairs.

Curtailed by the customers, Rory shook his head at Lyle. 'I'll get you back for that.'

Knowing they regularly wound each other up, Lyle wasn't concerned that his cousin's payback would be anything other than a playful gibe.

Skye and Ailsa had stopped near the vintage dress shop to chatter before going their separate ways.

Innis carefully placed a white and pale pink iced cake decorated with pink fondant flowers on a stand in the window display. He peered through the glow of the fairy lights at Skye chatting happily. There she was again, tugging at his heartstrings, pulling him in directions he wasn't sure he should go.

'I've scribbled some roughs for your shop's extension,' Rory's voice cut–in to Innis' thoughts.

Innis stepped back from the window and gave Rory his full attention.

Rory pointed to his notepad, showing a pencil sketch of a proposed extension to the back of the cake shop. 'This would give you room for about ten tables for customers to sit down to enjoy tea and cake.'

'That's exactly what I'm looking for. A part of the cake shop where customers can have morning and afternoon tea. I don't plan to be open in the evenings as I'm busy with the castle functions and my chocolatier work.'

'I've built extensions to quite a few shops in the main street, including Lyle's tea shop as you know. It's upstairs but the overall size is similar. But with your extension being in the garden, I could build it like a glass conservatory, making it light and airy. You could hang blinds on the windows to match your pink and yellow colour scheme, and pretty up your garden.'

'These are all great suggestions.' Innis sounded enthusiastic.

'You don't need a lot of fuss and fanciness. A lovely glass and light wood extension would do the business. Think it over.'

'I'm going to say yes. Start measuring it up. This is far better than I'd hoped for.'

Rory pulled out his tape measure from the pocket of his jeans. 'I'll measure it up and then give you an estimate of the cost. We'll take it from there. I'd suggest we don't start right in the middle of Christmastime. But I could make a start on it early in the New Year once the snow's gone. It won't take long to construct, and there will be minimal disruption to your cake shop. You won't have to close. I'll tackle the tricky and messy stuff before and after closing, and work away on the structuring during the day. I'll have it done in jig time, especially as Murdo's helping me.'

'Ideal.' Innis extended his hand to Rory. They shook hands.

'Right, I'll size up the garden.' Rory strode out the back door seeming to know exactly how to tackle the work.

Innis left him to it and went through to tell Rosabel and Primrose. He waited a moment while they finished serving customers and then confided his plans.

'We surmised as much when we saw Rory here,' Primrose said, smiling at him. 'It would be nice to have a wee tearoom area where folk could enjoy a cuppa and cake.'

'With silver cake stands, and pink and yellow linen napkins and accessories,' Rosabel added. 'We'd be

84

happy to serve it up. You wouldn't need extra staff unless it got awfy busy.'

'Between the three of us, I think we can manage,' Innis agreed.

'When do you plan to open it?' said Primrose.

'Rory says he'll make a start in the New Year after the snow has melted.'

'How exciting. I can picture it...all fancy cakes and chocolates and pretty pots of tea.'

Finlay and Ean sat with Nairne discussing the menu for the ball. Murdo had collected Lyle's book and Nairne flicked through it, reading Lyle's notes as he did so.

'This is a handy reference for the buffet,' said Nairne. 'We're used to catering for large functions, but it's always good to get some fresh ideas. Lyle has highlighted a few aspects that we could use.'

Finlay and Ean leaned forward as Nairne read out the details of everything from miniature quiche with cherry tomatoes to gingerbread cupcakes swirled with buttercream and decorated with fondant snowflakes.

'A lot of these are ideal for the finger buffet,' Finlay observed. 'And we'll have staff on hand to serve other items to the guests.'

'We'll include the hotplates with all the popular vegetables — roast potatoes, carrots, parsnips, traditional items. Then the roasts and salmon dishes,' Nairne added.

Happily chatting about the buffet menu, they continued until almost lunchtime when Finlay took a call from Merrilees.

She was at stargazer cottage working on her novel. 'Ed just phoned.' Ed, Edward, was her editor at the newspaper. 'He's read the editorial for the advertising feature and is running it in the entertainments section of tomorrow's paper, so it'll go to press tonight. He wants a photo to go with it. I'd suggest one from a recent party event at the castle. You have those on your website. I've messaged you with a picture I think would suit the feature.'

Finlay checked his phone. 'Yes, go with that. Great choice.'

'I'll send it to him right now.'

'Thanks, Merrilees,' said Finlay. 'We're planning the buffet menu.'

'I mentioned that ice cream delights were on the menu at the ball, along with delicious traditional recipes and Innis' chocolatier specialities.'

'That covers everything we need for now,' Innis confirmed.

'Okay, I'll get the pic to Ed so he can give the feature to the sub to do the layout for tonight's issue.'

'Are you coming up for dinner to the castle this evening?' Finlay said to her.

'Yes, see you around seven.'

Finlay put his phone away with a smile in his heart, looking forward to having dinner with Merrilees.

Stargazer cottage was cosy, but Merrilees had been writing since breakfast early in the morning, so after sending the photo to Ed, she put her warm jacket on and went out for a walk and a breath of fresh air.

The wind had a real bite to it, colder than the previous day, and above her the light grey clouds seemed to have a tinge of pink in their depths. She breathed in the sea air that rose up from the coast, but today it was challenged by the onslaught of gusts from inland that blew over from thistle loch. Was there a storm brewing? A thunderstorm perhaps?

Not venturing far from the cottage in case of a downpour, she walked through the long grass and hardy wild flowers that refused to give up the battle against the winter.

The long stems of the sea rocket plants and thistles bent with the wind and then bobbed back up defiant to full height. Like them, Merrilees marched on, filling her lungs with fresh air, hoping it would revive her senses and clear her head so she could continue writing like blazes when she got back to the cottage.

Dinner with Finlay was something to look forward to. It had crossed her mind to cook for the two of them and invite him over for dinner. She didn't do this often enough, but the offer of dinner at the castle suited her work schedule today as she could write until it was time to head there in the evening.

Working to deadlines at the newspaper had trained her to work fast and efficiently. A benefit when it came to writing her novel. She'd almost finished it. She just needed quiet time to create the romantic ending she needed to then send it to her publisher. A romantic ending is what she wished for with Finlay, and in her heart she sensed this would happen. But not yet, not in the midst of the hectic festive season.

A gust of wind almost blew her off her feet and she decided she'd had enough fresh air for now and walked briskly back home.

The welcoming warmth of the cottage soothed her senses, and after making a cup of tea, she settled down again beside the log fire with her laptop to type the day away.

Skye sat at her pink sewing machine in the vintage dress shop creating a full organza skirt to add to one of the evening dresses that had arrived earlier. She'd matched the colour of the pale cream organza that had flecks of gold to the oyster satin fabric.

'That looks lovely,' Holly commented, peering over at it.

'I'm fitting it to the bodice. The organza is quite firm so it'll sit out nicely over the dress.'

While Skye worked on the dress, Holly checked the online orders.

'Good news!' said Holly. 'We've had a message from our suppliers. They've posted half of the ball gowns to us and they'll arrive tomorrow.'

'Wonderful.'

'They're busy packing the other ball gowns and they're due the day after,' Holly explained.

'Perfect. It'll give us time to sort through the first lot.'

'Should I order in more organza, chiffon and tulle?' Holly looked at the list of ball gowns that were due to arrive, and took into account the evening dresses they'd received.

'Yes. Buy white, light cream, and the main pastel shades, especially if they're shot through with sparkle or metallic threads.'

Holly looked up a previous order. 'This is what we ordered a few months ago. We liked the quality of the fabric and the cost is very reasonable. They've even got a sale on.'

'Snap it up. We are going to need it.' Skye sounded sure and determined. 'Merrilees wants a ball gown. Obviously so do we, and Ailsa. But you know that others from the knitting bee will want one too, including Elspeth, Morven, Rowen, Rosabel and Primrose.' Skye smiled. 'I think we're going to be up to our tiaras in ball gown fashion and frou–frou.'

Holly laughed. 'You're slowly disappearing under all that organza.'

Skye grinned. 'Give me a hand will you so I can feed this part of the hem through the machine.'

Holly held the ends of the organza up while Skye stitched it.

'You're a whiz with that sewing machine,' Holly told her.

Skye laughed. 'Hold on tight, I'm coming to a tricky bit...okay, done!' She snipped the ends of the threads and secured them. Then she held the dress up.

'It's glittering under the lights.'

'I'm going to try it on and see how it looks.' Skye took the dress over to the changing room.

'I'll order more rolls of wired ribbon,' Holly called through to her. 'They've got sheer gold organza ribbon with glitter, and in silver...and pink!'

'Buy those,' said Skye. 'And any sparkling wired or stiff ribbon that would sit up beautifully on shoulder bows.'

Holly clicked the ribbon order, adding velvet ribbon too, something they used a lot of especially when mending pre–loved dresses. The ribbon was handy for hiding slight wear and tear and strengthening the mending. Many of the tea dresses they sold were repaired with ribbon and embroidery such as flowers.

They'd sold all the vintage dresses they'd shown at the fashion show, including the tartan taffeta ball gown.

Now with the festive season upon them, they'd ordered in evening dresses for the Christmas Eve dinner dance at the castle. But ball gowns would soon become popular at their shop.

Skye stepped out of the changing room. 'What do you think?'

'It's gorgeous.'

'It feels wonderful.' Skye viewed herself in the mirror. 'But I'm still holding out for the pink ball gown.' She went back in and got changed out of the dress and hung it up on a rail. 'One done, lots more to do.'

Holly checked the time. 'It's well after lunch. We're firing up on a scone and jam and cups of tea. Want to have those cheese and salad rolls you bought?'

'I could do with something tasty to eat, and a cuppa.' Skye went through to the kitchen at the back of the shop, put the kettle on and set the plates up.

Skye made the tea while Holly finished the orders, and then they sat at the kitchen table having a late lunch.

'Do you think Innis will invite you to the ball?' said Holly.

Skye shrugged. 'I don't know.' She had no idea.

Pinned up on the wall was a leaflet showing all the local activities that were part of the small town's Christmas celebrations.

Holly referenced the first item on the list. 'Are we going to the carol singing event tonight? Ailsa says people gather around the town's Christmas tree and sing, drink hot chocolate, toast marshmallows. As this is our first Christmas here owning the shop, it would be fun to go.'

'Hot chocolate, marshmallows and festive fun...yes, let's go.' Skye sipped her tea and eyed the other activities on the list. 'The Christmas market starts tomorrow and goes on for a couple of days. That sounds like fun too.'

'Ailsa has a stall and so does Rowen selling her yarn.'

'Do we need to take part?'

'No, it's mainly for local crafters or craft shops like Ailsa's shop. And the farmers sell their produce,' Holly explained. She checked the times. 'It's on from mid–morning until early evening.'

There was a picture of the previous year's Christmas market with all the stalls lit up at night.

'It looks so pretty. We should go in the evening,' said Skye, sounding enthusiastic. 'I love Christmas markets.' She'd only ever been to them in the cities, but she pictured they'd be similar and the town had plenty of crafters.

Working their way down the list, including events at the local restaurants and bars, including Brodrick's cafe bar Christmas nights, they saw that Lyle had a traditional festive tea offering Christmas cake, his special Yule log, scones and sandwiches one evening at his tea shop.

'We should go to Lyle's tea shop for that,' Holly insisted. 'An alternative to dinner.'

'A delicious alternative,' Skye agreed. 'Do we need to book a table?'

'It doesn't say. I'll check his website.' Holly looked up the events on the tea shop website and read what it said. *'Bookings are advised as it's a popular evening.'*

'Book a table for us.'

'Done,' Holly confirmed, and put her phone down to continue eating her sandwich. 'I hope Lyle has sandwiches as tasty as this one.'

Skye nodded, tucking into hers.

Giggling, they continued to plan their festive fun.

'I've never heard of this one.' Holly pointed to a lantern night at the forget–me–not waterfall.

'What do we have to do?'

'It doesn't say. Everyone except us will know so it'll be easy to find out,' said Holly. 'But I'm guessing it's bring a lantern to the waterfall and enjoy it all lit up.'

'Do you think we'll need our swimsuits?'

Holly's green eyes looked directly at Skye. 'Winter. Freezing. Ice cold water. I don't think so.'

'Maybe it's some sort of double dare challenge,' Skye said lightly. 'Skimpy dipping by moonlight.'

Holly laughed. 'Is that the demure version of skinny dipping?'

'It's my version.' Then she had second thoughts. 'But it would be freezing. Perhaps I'll just dangle a lantern and watch others brave it out.'

'It sounds nice though whatever it is. The waterfall is magical lit with those solar lights. Picture it if everyone has brought a lantern.'

'I love lanterns.' Skye recalled the little night light that she used to have by her bedside that she lit on stormy nights. 'But we don't have any.'

'Christmas market,' Holly said, looking like it was bound to have lanterns on sale.

'Okay, so we're going on the lantern night at the waterfall. What else is there?'

'Sledding near thistle loch.'

Their faces lit up with joyous mischief.

'Oh yes, we're doing that,' Skye sounded excited. 'It's just before the fairytale ball on Christmas Eve, so it'll have been snowing by then. The hills and countryside around the loch will be covered in snow.'

Delighted with the line–up of festive fun, they finished their lunch and then continued working on the dresses, repairing some and making others into gowns fit for the ball.

Finlay needed to update the castle's website. He phoned Innis at the cake shop. It was common practice for Finlay, Ean and Innis to all agree on important aspects when it came to the running of the castle.

'Ean and I have put together an update for the festive events at the castle,' Finlay explained. 'Enquires for the ball have been coming in already. We thought we could list it as we would the Christmas Eve dinner dance, but name it the Fairytale Ball. Add some of the editorial that Merrilees wrote for the newspaper, mentioning the lavish buffet and ballroom size function room. Dress to impress. That sort of thing. What do you think?'

'That sounds ideal. We've had customers coming into the cake shop asking about the ball too, so the sooner we list it the better,' said Innis. 'Rosabel and Primrose have been fending off the enquires to let me get on with my baking.'

'Merrilees says the feature will be in tomorrow's newspaper. I could update the information on our website this afternoon.'

'Do it.'

After finishing the call, Innis put the large Christmas cake he'd made in the window display. He'd decorated it with white icing, added sprigs of fondant holly and berries, and tied a red bow around the edges.

As he placed it in the window, he looked out and saw Holly heading to the post office with the day's orders. The parcels contained various vintage dresses including tea dresses and long sleeve wrap dresses that were proving popular for the winter.

Grabbing the opportunity to talk to Skye on her own, Innis hurried out, casting a comment to Rosabel and Primrose over his shoulder. 'I won't be long.'

Packing strawberry and vanilla butterfly cakes for customers, Rosabel and Primrose nudged each other as they stood behind the counter and shared a knowing smile.

CHAPTER SEVEN

Skye worked at her sewing machine in the vintage dress shop hemming one of the evening dresses. The design had a layer of ice blue chiffon sprinkled with sparkle, another contender for the ball gown collection. Repairing a hem was an easy enough task and it could make a prc–worn dress look refreshed again.

With the sound of the machine whirring away, she didn't hear the shop door open as Innis walked in.

He stood there for a moment watching her skilfully feed the fabric through the machine, clearly adept at this sort of mending.

'Skye.' His voice was a rich purr that caught her attention without jarring her.

She stopped sewing instantly and looked round at him, surprised to see him standing there so tall and handsome, making the shop appear smaller.

'I don't want to interrupt your work,' he began, but then he realised this was exactly what he was doing. *Fool*, he chided himself.

'It's fine,' she assured him with a smile and tilted her head, curious to know why he was there. He wore his usual work attire, a short sleeve white shirt and black trousers that showed his build to advantage. Her senses reacted in all sorts of ways that she hoped she hid well. Putting the dress on the sewing table, she stood up and gave him her full attention. Judging by him standing in her shop she reckoned he merited it. 'What can I do for you, Innis?'

Oh that he could answer that truthfully. Could she go with him to the ball? Could she realise how much he liked her and that he wanted to build on the brief momentum they'd exchanged at the fashion show? Could she understand the double–edged sword that cut through his heart every time he saw her? On one edge he wanted to ask her to be his girlfriend, and more. A lot more. On the other edge was the doubt that he could ruin her trusting heart, break it, even if unintentionally.

'Are you okay?' Her words jolted him from his conflicting thoughts.

'Yes, well...I wanted to...' What? Take her in his arms and kiss the breath from her? Feeling he couldn't just ask her to start dating him, beginning with the ball, he side–stepped the situation of his own making and commented on her dressmaking. 'Is that one of the new ball gowns you're sewing?' Then he reworded this. 'Not new obviously, but vintage...what is it you call them...pre–loved?'

Skye's expression brightened even more. He'd taken an interest. 'Yes, that's right.' She held up part of the dress showing him how the blue chiffon sparkled under the shop lights. 'This arrived with the evening dresses, but I think it's lovely enough to be one of the ball gowns. I'm mending the hem. The fabric is chiffon so I'm using a rolled hem technique to keep the edges fluid.'

Was she babbling? She hoped not, but he wasn't fidgeting or looking bored. He looked interested in what she was telling him.

'It looks beautiful.' So did Skye.

She paused, holding her gaze steady with his, wondering what he wanted. He never dropped by for a casual chat. Nothing about Innis was ever casual. So why was he here?

'Were the chocolates to your liking?' he said finally.

Realising she hadn't commented on them, and he probably valued feedback, she replied with enthusiasm. 'Yes, they were delicious. I tried two or three. They were all very nice. I particularly liked the toffee cup sprinkled with white chocolate like snow, the dark truffle and the spicy Christmas flavoured one.' She giggled. 'All of them really. The other ladies at the knitting bee said you were scrumptious too.'

He smiled.

'No, not you, what I mean is...your new chocolates.' The blush she'd been fighting to keep down rose up in all its telltale glory.

He cut–in to rescue her from her embarrassing remark. 'I'm glad. Feedback from people that I can rely on to be honest with me is very helpful.'

Skye nodded and drew breath. Change the subject to anything and calm down, she scolded herself. 'Are you going to the carol singing this evening?'

He looked like he knew nothing about it.

Scooting past him into the kitchen, she was going to pull the leaflet off the wall to show him the list of events when she felt him standing in the kitchen doorway, his shoulders filling the width of it and tapering down to that lean torso.

'This is the list of local events this Christmastime.' She gestured to the leaflet and moved aside a little so that he could have a peek.

He stepped closer to read it, closer to her.

She didn't want to step back in case he thought she was trying to avoid him or create any awkwardness. The turmoil in her stomach was enough to make her feel like she was on the brink of acting like a complete fool. Maybe she was already. With the mix of emotions flooding through her, it was hard to gauge if she was fooling anyone, including herself.

Those amber eyes scanned the list, taking in each one, while Skye took him in, so close and yet so far.

They'd danced at the fashion show, so she knew what it felt like to be wrapped in his strong arms. But he'd never been in her kitchen or her shop like this, so informal, when it was just the two of them. Was he really here to get feedback on his chocolates? Innis wasn't easy to read. That guard of his was always up. But here he was, standing right there reading the leaflet like it interested him immensely.

'I'd no idea there were so many events this year.' He sounded genuine.

'I think there are more than ever. The recent publicity in the newspapers in Glasgow has sparked interest in the island. A few of the knitting bee ladies have said they've had more customer enquires and sales for their crafts than previous years.' She shrugged. 'So I'm guessing that more events have been added to cater for visitors. Though I'm happy with everything that's listed and hope to attend most of them.'

'Even the sledging?' His lips curved into a wry smile.

'Especially the sledging. I know I don't look like the daring type, but just watch me. Those slopes are going to be well used by me.'

His smile reached up to his intense amber eyes framed with dark lashes that added to his wolfish persona. 'I might take you up on that challenge.'

Skye blinked. 'Challenge? I wasn't actually—'

He shrugged his shoulders, and she saw his strong chest peeking out from the unbuttoned top of his shirt. 'It sounded like a challenge to me.'

He was teasing her surely. Wasn't he? She perked up, and the mischief element in her nature kicked in. 'Okay. See you on the slopes.'

'Do you have a sledge?'

'No, but that can be remedied. There's a Christmas market tomorrow and Holly and I are buying lamps for the lantern walk event. There are probably sledges on sale too. If not, I'll ask Ailsa if she can order them for us from her craft shop.'

'The castle has sledges,' he told her. These were for the use of guests, though Innis and his brothers had long enjoyed the sledging, with or without an official event.

Skye put her hands on her hips and gave him a challenging look. 'It's okay for some people.'

'I'll put two aside for you and Holly. But be warned. They're designed for speed.' He was winding her up.

Skye took the bait. 'All the better to beat you with Mr Wolf.' The words were out before she could filter them.

He grinned. 'I'm looking forward to our race.'

He was playing with her. But was he flirting? Was Innis capable for flirting? Before she could decide, he referenced the other events on the list.

'The carols and hot chocolate event this evening sound enticing, but I have plans for tonight.' This including taking a walk up into the hills after closing the cake shop. He had a lot on his mind that needed consideration and he always thought clearly when he walked up there in the evenings.

'Baking and business,' she summarised.

'Yes, I'm planning to try out new recipes for my chocolates, working late in the castle kitchen,' he explained.

Skye tilted her head in genuine awe. 'I can't imagine how you make all those smooth, beautiful chocolates. They look like they've been manufactured by a top confectionary company. But they have your handcrafted mastery.'

She didn't intend to flatter him, and this flattered him all the more. Hearing her opinion of his chocolatier work meant more to him than he realised. Dropping his guard for a moment, the invitation was out before he could reconsider it. 'Come up to the castle this evening and see how they're made.'

Skye found herself nodding and yet she'd told Holly she'd go to the carol singing.

His mind took this into account. 'I'll be working quite late. You're welcome to pop up after the carols

101

and hot chocolate with marshmallows.' He'd glimpsed what was included in the event.

'Yes, I will. I'll go easy on the hot chocolate if I've to indulge in eating your chocolates. I'm assuming I'll be your official taster?'

He hadn't thought of this, but lied and planned to make it so if she came and joined him later that evening. 'Yes, you can sample the new flavours.'

She'd been joking, playing along with their light banter, experiencing a side he'd kept hidden for so long. 'I promise not to eat all your chocolates.'

'You can have anything you want from me, Skye.'

The richness of his tone sent shivers through her, nervous shivers of romantic excitement.

'I'll see you tonight at the castle,' she confirmed, needing him to leave now so she could breathe and think about the potential trouble she'd entrenched herself in. Not that she was complaining. She loved a challenge. And she'd a feeling that Innis and his chocolatier work that evening at the castle would be far more challenging than the snowy slopes.

He walked through to the shop, needing to get back to his own work too.

Before leaving he offered her a lift to the castle. 'Would you like me to pick you up this evening?'

'No, I'll drive myself there. It'll let you keep working without interruption. You'll have enough of that to contend with when I arrive to chomp your chocolates.'

She made him smile. And she made something in him feel alive, as if he was glad he'd overstepped his own mark and invited her to join him while he worked on his chocolates.

'I'll see you later,' he said and left, leaving her stunned that she sort of had a date night arranged with Innis.

She sat back down at her sewing machine and didn't stitch anything. Flopping back in her chair she wondered what she'd cornered herself into. Not only the chocolatier experience later on, but the sledging.

Although she wasn't inclined to be nervous when it came to social events, she felt the anticipation of an evening with Innis flutter through her stomach.

'Was that Innis I saw leaving the shop?' Holly's voice shook her from her thoughts.

'Yes, he was here to get feedback on the box of chocolates he gave me.'

Skye's words hung in the air so heavy that Holly knew something had happened. And she saw the rosy glow across her sister's cheeks.

'You look flushed.'

Skye's blue eyes were filled with trepidation. 'I've sort of challenged Innis on the snow slopes. He's lending us sledges from the castle. They're fast, apparently.'

'You've never done sledging.' Neither had Holly, but she wasn't taking on the wolf.

'No, but—'

'Innis will have been sledging since he was a boy. How to you plan to win?' Holly knew Skye was competitive, but nevertheless...

'Skulduggery, mischief and bamboozlement.' Skye pressed her lips together and nodded firmly, trying to

103

convince herself about her tactics. They were the first tactics that sprang to mind, but often impulsiveness worked well for her.

Holly had seen Skye's mischievous character succeed before. 'It sounds like you're in with a chance.'

They giggled.

'And he's invited me to the castle tonight to taste his new range of chocolates and see his chocolatier skills.' Skye explained the details.

Holly smiled and shook her head. 'I leave you for ten minutes while I pop to the post office and when I come back you've wangled two dates with Innis.'

'Wangled is right. I don't think he had any intention of asking me to do either.' She frowned. 'Though he seemed out of sorts, like he was making up an excuse, wanting to know what I thought about the new chocolates. I think he was edgy, as if he'd dashed in on the spur of the moment. Maybe he'd seen you leaving and thought he could chat to me for a few minutes on my own. I don't know.' She swept the wisps of hair from her pinned up messy pleats that were threatening to unravel, almost as much as she was.

'That makes sense,' Holly said firmly. 'The two of you are never alone together. He probably did see me head to the post office. He sees everything from his cake shop window, and he couldn't miss me laden with parcels for posting.'

Skye agreed. 'Whenever I'm in his cake shop, Rosabel and Primrose are there too. So, you're right. We don't have many private moments.'

104

'And Innis is the deep, secretive sort. He's not like Rory or Lyle. Rory would march in and ask you to go out with him in front of a crowd, totally unabashed. Lyle's no shrinking violet either when it comes to speaking up.'

'Well, now all I have to do is settle my own jitters until I drive up to the castle.'

'I'll put the kettle on for tea. And you can sing your heart out before you go. You can't sing Christmas carols and have the jitters at the same time.'

'Is that true?'

Holly hustled through to the kitchen and filled the kettle. 'Maybe, probably,' she called through to Skye.

'What will I wear?' Skye eyed the clothes rails, suddenly spoiled for choice, though a glamorous dress wouldn't be suitable.

'Go glamorous,' Holly advised, rattling around in the kitchen, hoping they hadn't eaten the last of the shortbread.

'A glamorous evening dress isn't appropriate.'

'You don't need to wear an evening dress to be glam. Emphasise your assets. Wear a pair of those stretch velvet trousers that flatter you so well.'

'The dark blue ones or the burgundy?'

'Burgundy. And wear that lovely cropped white jumper you knitted. You look great in it.'

'That could work. Not too overdressed, but suitable for the winter.'

'And textures that will tempt him.'

'I'm not aiming to tempt Innis tonight.'

Holly guffawed. 'Keep telling yourself that.'

Skye relented. 'Okay, maybe it would be nice to see if the spark I felt the last time I was dancing with him could be reignited.'

'But be careful. You're playing with fire if you play around with Innis.'

'What! You're the one encouraging me.'

The kettle clicked off and Holly busied herself making the tea. 'I'm just reminding you to keep your guard up. Feel things out. You'll know if he's toying with you. Though I don't think he's the type. Rosabel and Primrose think he's ready to settle down.'

Skye sat down at the kitchen table and cupped her hands around her mug of tea. 'Settle as in...'

'All in. Perhaps Innis will be the first of the three brothers to get engaged.'

There was no shortbread left so they drank their tea.

'Can't I just go for a fun night of eating chocolates at the castle?'

Holly shrugged. 'That's an option, but let's see what the night brings. And you've got a back–up plan.'

Skye didn't know what it was. 'I have?'

'The sledging,' Holly told her. 'Skulduggery, mischief and what else was it?'

'Bamboozlement.' Skye started to smile as she said this.

Laughing and drinking their tea, they talked about Skye's date with Innis and wondered how the night would unfold.

Innis finished icing the cakes he'd been working on while avoiding the inquisitive looks from Rosabel and Primrose. They'd seen him popping into the vintage dress shop and knew that Holly was at the post office.

'I wanted to know if Skye liked my new selection of chocolates,' he eventually relented.

'Did she?' Rosabel prompted him while rearranging the bon bons in one of the display cabinets.

'Yes, especially the toffee cups, dark truffles and Christmas spice flavour,' he elaborated to show that they really had been discussing his confectionary. The gossip about him inviting Skye to the castle would be rife tomorrow, but he wanted a little bit of breathing space before that started circulating.

'He's hiding something,' Rosabel murmured to Primrose.

'We'll find out later,' Primrose whispered to Rosabel. 'Holly and Skye are going to the carol singing. Holly told me.'

'He's definitely got a spring in his step,' Rosabel observed, watching Innis move deftly around the kitchen and dart back and forth to the window display to add more cakes.

'I heard that,' Innis said, causing them to giggle.

Yes, he thought. The gossip was going to be sensational. He hoped it would be worth it. Skye certainly was. He probably did have a spring in his step even though it was the depth of winter.

After Rosabel and Primrose left the shop at the end of the working day, he tidied up, he put on his sturdy walking boots so he could trudge up into the hills.

Shrugging on his warm jacket, he flicked the main lights off, leaving the window display aglow with fairy lights, and strode off up into the hills as the early evening sky deepened.

The cold wind blew through his thick dark hair, emphasising his sculptured profile as he forged on up the steep slope. This was the fastest route to the top, and the toughest, but over the years his strong, lean thighs had become accustomed to the attempted assault on his muscles. He didn't feel the burn these days, and hadn't for a long time. The hill walking was one of the things he believed kept him fit and strong.

At the top, he was usually the lone figure, standing there, looking out at the island below and other islands way off in the distance. The sea and the sky merged at different points around the curve of the long, sweeping bay. The seasons were at their most distinguishable from his vantage point.

Gazing up at the darkening sky, he saw snowflakes flutter through the air. They were there and gone in seconds.

The scent of snow in the icy air was unmistakable. Here it comes, he thought with assurance. The snow was on its way tonight.

He glanced down to where the festive lights outlined the main street edging the bay. Often the lights were crystal clear, but this year they glowed with colourful red, green, pink, blue and golden yellow.

The little fire pit they'd set up to toast marshmallows flickered with warmth.

The large Christmas tree adorned with a star on top shone like a beacon. Skye would be there singing carols, but later she'd be driving up to the castle. The roads were at their most unpredictable when the first fall of snow occurred. Once everything was covered in snow the roads were strangely more reliable. Should he warn her to be extra careful? Or would that seem like he was fussing?

Deciding that Skye was a competent young woman capable of handling the drive, he tried to listen to the carol singing. The voices were barely audible, but the wintry breeze blew a few notes up into the hills. Traditional songs from yesteryear rose up and touched his heart, reminding him of all that made Christmas special. Though this year, Skye was the true heart of it for him.

Murdo lugged a couple of sledges across the castle's front lawn as Merrilees arrived for dinner with Finlay.

She parked her car and called over to Murdo. 'Isn't it a bit early for sledging?'

'Innis wanted me to bring them out of the garden shed where we keep them. I'm taking them round to the storeroom to give them a buff and spruce up for Skye and Holly.'

'Are they using them for props for their dress shop modelling photos?' She couldn't think why else they'd want them.

'No, they're for hitting the slopes for the sledging event.'

The journalist in her was intrigued. 'But there's no snow forecast yet, and the sledging isn't until just before Christmas Eve.' Having written about the list of events on the island for the newspaper, she was familiar with the schedule.

Murdo shrugged. 'Innis didn't elaborate. He was busy frosting a fruit cake and it was a quick call to get me to earmark these for Skye and Holly.' He smiled and continued on his way, trailing them round to the storeroom at the back of the castle.

Merrilees headed inside reception and was greeted by Finlay as he stood behind the desk discussing the dinner menu with Geneen.

'I hope you're hungry,' Finlay said to Merrilees, walking round and giving her a welcoming hug. 'Chef has exceeded himself this evening. He's practising items for the ball's buffet.'

'Yes, I am.' She'd barely stopped writing all day, forging on, knowing that dinner was at the end of it. Cups of tea and a shortbread finger had kept her going while she wrote by the fireside in stargazer cottage.

'Wonderful.' Finlay put his arm around her shoulder and escorted her through to their usual private table in the far corner of the function room.

She mentioned about Murdo and the sledges.

It was the first he'd heard of this.

'Why does Innis want sledges put aside for Skye and Holly?' said Merrilees.

'I don't know, but I'm sure he'll tell me what he's up to when he comes home to the castle this evening,' Finlay concluded.

Nairne fussed around Finlay and Merrilees as staff served up samples from the buffet menu.

They both tried the grilled Scottish salmon pastries with caramelised red onions and a medley of roast vegetables flavoured with peppers and tomatoes.

Finlay gestured to his plate. 'Everything in this selection should be served at the ball's buffet.'

Merrilees was in agreement.

Pleased that they approved, Nairne headed back through to the kitchen. Innis was due back soon to commandeer his area of the kitchen for his chocolatier work. Nairne wanted to make everything tidy for his arrival. He'd no idea that Skye would be joining Innis later. Innis rarely invited anyone to watch him work on his confectionary.

Skye and Holly were wrapped up warm against the cold night as they joined in the carol singing.

Skye's long hair tumbled around the shoulders of her pastel pink wool coat. A retro buy from the seventies that had become one of her favourites. She wore a woolly white hat and mittens that she'd knitted herself. The white yarn had a light sparkle effect through it and she'd bought skeins of it from Elspeth and Morven's knitting shop. Under her coat she wore the burgundy velvet trousers tucked into boots, and the white jumper. She'd fussed with her makeup and was feeling butterflies of excitement about her so–called date with Innis.

Singing took her mind off the impending evening at the castle as she concentrated on the song sheet.

Standing beside Holly near the large Christmas tree, she felt the heat from the fire where marshmallows were being toasted. The flames

111

flickered against the backdrop of the shimmering silvery sea, creating the perfect atmosphere for the festive singing.

This was such a wonderful lifestyle here on the island, Skye thought. She didn't miss the mainland or the cities, and neither did Holly. They'd settled into their new and exciting life on the island. The only thing that was missing for both of them was romance. There was no one that Holly had in mind. And only one man that Skye considered getting involved with. But Innis...well, he was such a lone wolf. Would he be the man for her?

Holly wore grey cords with boots, a beige Aran jumper, a cream wool coat and matching cream woolly hat, gloves and scarf. The scarf was red and she'd knitted her accessories herself.

'Hello, ladies,' a man's familiar voice said, approaching them from his tea shop.

'Lyle.' Holly was the first to react with a smile, shortly followed by Skye.

'Are you here for the singing or the hot chocolate and marshmallows?' Holly said to him.

Before he could explain, one of the main organisers of the carol singing saw Lyle and made an announcement. The man's voice sounded clear in the cold night air.

'I'd like to thank Lyle for contributing all the hot chocolate and marshmallows for tonight's event,' the man announced, causing everyone to acknowledge Lyle's kindness with smiles and a round of applause.

'I'm happy to help out,' Lyle told them, giving a cheery wave.

Holly looked at him. 'You provided the hot chocolate and marshmallows?' She didn't mean to sound so surprised.

'Yes, the local folk support my tea shop so I wanted to give a wee bit back to help with the event,' he explained. 'Other businesses are contributing to the festive events this year,' he added, giving credit to others. 'Innis has given large boxes of his luxury chocolates for the raffles, and cakes. I've given an iced fruit cake, a Christmas cake for a raffle at tomorrow's market. Make sure to buy a ticket. You never know your luck.' His cheerful manner made them smile warmly at him.

'We will,' said Holly.

'Right, I'm away back to my tea shop,' he said, rubbing his hands together for warmth. He'd thrown a jacket on but the biting cold blowing in from the sea made him shiver. 'Enjoy your hot chocolate.'

'I'm forgoing it,' said Skye, unable to contain her news. 'Innis has invited me up to the castle to show me how he makes his chocolates.'

Lyle's face lit up with a smile. 'Ooooh! A date night?'

Skye raised her shoulders and tucked her hands deep into her coat pockets. 'I'm not sure.'

'Ah, that's Innis for you. Sometimes you never quite know where you stand,' said Lyle. 'But for all his lone wolf and standoffish tendencies, I find him to be a good–hearted man. Maybe not the easiest to get along with, but...Innis and his brothers are generous to a fault when it comes to the local community.'

'A wee bit like yourself, Lyle.'

Holly's remark made him feel the unfamiliar sense of a blush rising up. 'No, I wouldn't put myself in their league.'

Flakes of snow started to fall around them.

'Innis was right,' Lyle was the first to remark. 'The snow is early this winter.'

'Will it start with a light covering of snow?' said Skye.

'No, once it starts snowing this evening, it'll be a whiteout by midnight and that'll be the last you'll see of the greenery on the hills until the thaw in the New Year,' Lyle explained.

'Perhaps I should drive up to the castle now before it becomes too heavy,' Skye suggested.

'Yes, but drive slow and steady,' Lyle advised.

'I will,' said Skye. Hurrying away, she gave a cheery wave to Holly and Lyle, got into the car she shared with her sister that was parked outside their dress shop, and drove off.

It was Holly's turn to shiver.

'Get yourself a hot drink. You're looking a wee bitty cold,' Lyle advised her.

'I will. I'm probably needing something to eat, so I'll indulge in plenty of marshmallows.'

'Have you not had dinner?'

'No, we were working late at the shop, and then it was a flurry of getting ready for the carol singing. The time flew in and...here I am.'

Lyle thumbed behind him at his tea shop. 'I'm heading back for a bowl of soup that I've left simmering on the stove for my dinner. I've had enough sugary things today. I like to eat a hearty soup

114

made with plenty of winter vegetables. I add lentils or split peas to the mix. Tonight, it's split peas.'

Holly's tummy rumbled at the thought of it. It sounded tasty, but she didn't want to force him to invite her to join him.

'You're welcome to join me for a bowl of soup and crusty bread,' he offered. His offer was genuine, and he was under no illusion that this was a date night in the making with the beautiful Holly.

'Okay, thanks, that would be great.'

Walking together to his tea shop, they chatted about the ball gowns that were due to arrive the next morning. Or at least, Holly did, chattering happily.

He listened with interest.

Lyle was easy to talk to she thought as she headed out of the cold and into the cosy tea shop that smelled of a savoury dinner cooking.

The tea shop was closed for the evening, and he'd tidied the front shop area so everything looked shiny and clean. The fire still flickered in the hearth, creating a homely ambiance.

'Come on through to the kitchen,' he beckoned her. 'It's nice and toasty. I've had the ovens on baking cakes and cooking the soup on the stove.'

Holly followed him through, glad to be out of the cold and in the cosiness of the tea shop kitchen. The modern vintage styling was lovely and she admired the floral ceramic teapots on the shelves, along with the pretty blue and white stripe milk jugs. Shiny pots and pans hung on the walls and reflected the overhead spotlights.

He lifted the lid on the large pot that was simmering on the stove. 'Yes, it's ready. Let me take your coat.'

She took her coat and accessories off and he hung them up along with his jacket in a cupboard.

He gestured for her to sit down at the kitchen table while he washed his hands and then proceeded to serve up two bowls of the soup. He poured two ladles full each, sprinkled greentails on top, added a dash of freshly ground black pepper, and then selected a farmhouse loaf and cut thick slices for them.

And all the while Holly continued chatting about the ball gowns. 'The first half of the delivery arrives tomorrow. The suppliers are sending the second half, but it'll give us a chance to sort through the dresses and start getting them ready for sale.'

'Will you and Skye have the pick of them, or are some earmarked for customers?'

'Skye has her eye on a pink sparkly ball gown. Pink really is her colour and the dress is like something out of a fairytale, so that one is hers. I haven't decided yet which one I'd like. I know it sounds silly, but we're so excited to have all these wonderful dresses arriving. We had a delivery of evening dresses too, and it was like opening Christmas presents. Skye has already added organza and chiffon to a couple of the dresses so they're ideal now for the ball.'

'Tuck in,' he said, 'and help yourself to the bread.'

'Oh this is so tasty.' She enjoyed a couple of spoonfuls and then lifted a slice of bread and took a bite of it.

He continued their conversation about the dresses. 'When I picture a ball gown I think of something all sparkly and light. I don't know a lot about fabrics, but silk and chiffon comes to mind. What was that other fabric you mentioned?'

'Organza.'

'Is that like chiffon?'

'Yes, only chiffon is soft and fluid, but organza is a bit firmer so it sits out well for a ball gown.'

'I had to select various fabrics for the tea room furnishings. I found it interesting the way traditional patterns like floral prints and gingham are still popular.' He pointed to the kitchen curtains. 'I chose that yellow and white cotton gingham for the curtains. It makes the kitchen look sunny even on dull days or dark mornings when I'm in here early to start baking fresh scones and cakes.'

'You work long hours, but I never hear you complain about being tired. You're always cheery when I come into your tea shop.'

'That's because I love what I do. I'm where I want to be, doing what I've always wanted. The tea shop has thrived beyond my expectations. Yes, it's hard work, but I'm sure you feel the same about your vintage dresses and fashions.'

'I do. Sometimes I'm reluctant to leave the shop if I'm working on a dress, repairing it, adding special touches that bring the past up–to–date. I forget the time and just keep sewing and mending until it's done. But like you I don't feel tired because I love my work. I've loved fashion and dresses since I was a wee girl. And so has Skye.'

117

A message came through on Holly's phone. 'Sorry, I have to check this in case it's Skye.' She read the message and smiled. 'Skye's arrived at the castle. It's snowing heavy up in the forest. But she's safe.' She tucked her phone away and relaxed, happy to continue enjoying her time with Lyle.

'I hope things work out well between Skye and Innis,' he said.

'So do I. She's liked him for a while, and there's an obvious spark between them, but I worry she'll get her heart broken. And I worry too that she won't take a chance on love.' She sounded unsure.

'Skye's a sweetheart. She deserves to find romance and happiness. Hopefully, it'll be with Innis. As I said, he's a good man.'

'And handsome too.' She meant that he was a heartbreaker.

'Apparently, the most handsome man on the island.' Lyle wasn't as tall, handsome or imposing as Innis, but he was nonetheless a fine looking man with light brown hair and hazel eyes that twinkled with interest.

'Innis is a looker,' she said.

Lyle shrugged his broad shoulders. 'Good looks fade with time. But a kind heart remains constant.'

CHAPTER EIGHT

Innis was working in the castle kitchen, setting up everything he needed for making his chocolates. He'd changed into clean clothes and wore a black shirt version of the short sleeve white one.

Through the glass door that led from the kitchen out to the patio at the back of the castle, he could see the snow falling fast.

Declining to check the time, he started preparing the items for the new recipes, hoping Skye would turn up soon. Perhaps the snow had held her up, but she wasn't late by any means. He was just eager for her to arrive.

Nairne worked in the main part of the kitchen along with other staff, preparing food for the guests. This was normal practise. Innis often worked in his area of the kitchen without disturbing them.

Innis had prepared the tray of moulds for the individual chocolates, and had the tempered milk chocolate and cocoa butter at the ready. Mixing the consistency he needed in a bowl, he transferred it to a pastry piping bag and was about to pipe the smooth mixture into the moulds when Geneen walked in with Skye.

'Skye's here to see you, Innis,' Geneen announced. Smiling at Skye, she left them to enjoy their evening.

Geneen had taken Skye's coat and accessories at reception, so she stood there looking lovely in her velvet trousers and white jumper with her blonde hair rippling over her shoulders. Around her wrist was a bobble that she planned to use to tie her hair back if need be. She wasn't sure how the chocolate making demonstration would go or if she'd be involved in any of the mixing.

'It's snowing!' she said, breaking the ice as he paused from verbally welcoming her.

He heard his hesitation and hoped she didn't mistake it for a less than enthusiastic welcome. In his heart, he was admiring her. Sometimes, she looked so beautiful she took his breath away.

He glanced out at the deepening snowscene behind him. 'I trust it wasn't too difficult to drive here, especially through the forest.'

'No, it was quite exciting, like driving in a snowglobe.' She didn't have much experience of navigating snowy roads. In the city it turned to slush so quickly with the busy traffic, or snow ploughs had cleared the roads by the time she'd driven on them. She'd never ventured far north on the mainland during the depths of winter, so this was sort of her first time driving through it. 'I left the carol singing as soon as it started, but by the time I got to the forest road everything was covered in it.'

'It'll be like this throughout Christmas.'

'A white Christmas guaranteed.'

'Yes, the whole island sparkles with snow. The early morning views from the top of the hills is something to see. The evenings too when you can see the lights of the town. I saw the fire pit for the marshmallow toasting from my usual vantage point. I went for a walk before heading home here. I heard the singing too.'

'Holly and I joined in. It was fun. But I didn't have any hot chocolate or marshmallows.' She glanced at the chocolate he was preparing to pipe into the tray, and the scent of the chocolate filled the air.

'Would you like to grab an apron and help me?' he said.

Thrown right in at the deep end. 'Yes, I'll wash my hands first.' She saw that he had a separate sink in his area of the kitchen and tied her hair back in a ponytail while she walked over and washed her hands.

The amber eyes flickered, impressed by her attitude.

'Any experience of making sweets or confectionery?' he said as she unhooked a chef's white apron and put it on.

'No, but I've baked cakes.' She tied the straps and tried to look confident rather than show how nervous she was. You can do this, she bolstered herself. It's just chocolate. Making sweeties. And standing next to Innis as he instructed her.

'The moulds are prepared, and I've mixed the melted chocolate with a hint of spices and fruit flavouring. All you have to do is pipe it into the tray, like piping icing or buttercream on a cake.'

'I can do that.' She was confident she could. Swirling buttercream on cupcakes was something she did have experience of. Holly was usually in charge of baking the cakes and mixing the buttercream, but she'd helped with the topping.

Squeezing the bag too firmly, the melted chocolate splattered out of the tip.

121

'Easy does it,' Innis said, clasping her hands with his and guiding her as she filled a few of the little round moulds on the tray.

She hoped he didn't hear her heart thundering at his touch, and the closeness of his hard, lean body. He wasn't intentionally driving her to distraction. But oh my...her reaction to him was potent.

Concentrate on doing it right, she told herself, and somehow she held her nerve and filled the tray with only a couple of blobs that he wiped away.

'I'm impressed,' he said. 'It took me a lot of practice to get it right, and you did it first time.'

'Really?' Her eyes blinked at him, so close he could see the clear blue in their depths.

'Yes,' his tone was genuine. 'Perhaps it's your dressmaking skills coming into play. I'm sure you have to do a lot of finicky stitching that takes a steady hand.'

This made sense to Skye. 'I do, especially the embroidery work with its satin stitches, French knots and bullion knots, or sewing on sequins and beads. And putting in a new zip. Now that's tricky.'

He stepped back and nodded. 'Well then. I'll put you in charge of the piping while I make more of the mixture. Next up is the dark chocolate truffles.'

'What happens to this tray?'

'It's put aside over here to set. Once the chocolate is almost set, we'll pop a glacé cherry on top. You'll be in charge of the toppings.'

'What about the tasting?' she said teasingly.

'That comes after the chocolates are made. Work first, then pleasure.'

122

It wasn't his intention to send her heart racing, but the way he said *pleasure* ignited all sorts of feelings in her. Keeping her head down while she tamed the blush threatening to give the game away, she focussed on the chocolate making.

When it was time to pop the cherries on the chocolates, Skye paused. 'Are all the glacé cherries accounted for?' There was mischief in her tone.

Innis played along. 'Yes, but somehow a few always go missing.'

'Mmmm,' Skye mumbled. 'I wonder why?'

His lips formed a sexy grin as he let her steal a couple of the cherries, and then stole one himself.

Skye giggled. 'This is fun.'

His amber eyes gazed right at her. 'It is.' Two words that meant everything.

Being with Skye made him realise what was missing from his life. Her.

Hiding his feelings for her, Innis showed her how he created the fine chocolate shells and then added a variety of fillings. He made sure that each filling, ranging from fruit pastes to praline was the correct consistency before piping or spooning it into the shells.

She watched his skilful hands make each chocolate perfectly, and it was clear that this was something he enjoyed doing. Sometimes he lathered the tempered chocolate on to a marble slab and smoothed it with a spatula.

Everything from the thick creams and cocoa butter to the white, milk and dark chocolate, was selected and carefully mixed for each recipe.

'I never realised you used so many techniques to create your chocolates. It's quite an art in itself.'

He smiled at her compliment as he used a chocolate ganache mix to make the truffles and dipped them in melted chocolate. 'Would you like to help me roll the truffles in cocoa powder?'

'Yes, what do I have to do?'

Taking charge again of her hands, he gave her fine fork to roll each truffle in the cocoa. 'Roll the truffles in the cocoa and then carefully lift each one out and place them on the tray,' he instructed her.

It wasn't deliberate, but he couldn't help feel his hands brush against the softness of her jumper and her long ponytail. He tried to lean back rather than crowd her, but she seemed at ease with him and he sensed that perhaps she felt the sparks of attraction ignite when they were close.

Forcing herself to be competent rather than melt into his arms, as she longed to do, she made the chocolates as he instructed. The scent of the sweets was deliciously tempting — and so was Innis.

Did he know how strongly he affected her? Did he?

'Would you like a cup of tea while the chocolates firm and set?' he offered.

'Yes, thanks.'

He started to prepare the tea while she watched him. He always looked so capable when he was working in his cake shop, and it was the same in the castle kitchen. Boiling water was on hand and the tea was made quickly.

'Would you like something to eat?' He was thinking chocolates or cake.

'Please, anything would be great.'

He frowned. 'You've had dinner, haven't you?'

'No, I worked late at the shop and then went to the carol singing.' She wasn't angling for dinner.

Innis wished he'd offered her something when she arrived. He'd assumed she'd had dinner, but... 'What would you like to eat?' He got ready to make it for her.

'Don't go to any special bother. A sandwich would be lovely.'

Innis was having none of it and sat her down at the nearby table that had a view of the snow falling outside. 'Sit down here and have your tea. I'll be back in a moment.'

Striding over to the main kitchen area he mumbled something to Nairne and then they both selected a delicious platter of items from the buffet menu.

Innis carried the platter back over to her on a tray and put it down. A place setting, napkin and cutlery were swiftly arranged by him in front of her, and then the platter added.

'Is this suitable? Is it enough? I can make something else if you'd prefer.'

His offer was genuine and she liked him all the more for it.

'This is perfect, thank you. I didn't want to create any hassle. I should've had dinner but—'

'I should've offered when you arrived,' he cut–in. 'Now, relax and have something to eat. I'm going to grab something for myself too.' He went back over to

Nairne and returned with a platter, and sat down at the table with her.

'Did you miss out on dinner as well?' she said.

He nodded and bit into one of the mini quiche samples and then sipped his tea. 'I lingered up on the hills. Then it started to snow and I watched it change the view. I've always loved to see the snow coming. The way it blows in from the sea at night reminds me of starlight.'

She smiled warmly while tucking into her food. 'You sound like a romantic at heart.'

Had he revealed too much? Or was Skye reading him better than most?

He shrugged those broad shoulders that carried the weight of everything he was responsible for and concentrated on his meal.

Sensing he didn't want to discuss being romantic, she changed the subject. 'This cheese pastry is delicious.'

He'd done it again, he scolded himself. Pushed her away when he wanted the complete opposite effect. Steeling himself ready to reveal his feelings, he changed the subject back again. 'I'd like to be.'

She blinked, thrown by the changing conversation.

'Romantic.' His tone was deep and resonated through her.

'I'm sure you are, Innis.'

He smiled and nodded, and then they both continued to eat their food and find comfort in each other's company.

Lyle poured another cup of tea for Holly. They'd finished their soup and sat in the tea shop kitchen continuing to chat about their businesses and lives on the island. But he had a piece of unexpected news she didn't know about.

'I've bought a farmhouse near Rory's place,' he revealed. 'A fixer–upper. I asked Rory to keep a lookout for a property, and he found this for me. I purchased it last week and Rory's going to do it up. It's a bit rundown, but it'll be a fine house when it's finished.'

'How exciting!'

'I currently live with my parents. I love them to bits and we get on great. But it's time I got a house of my own and let them have the same. With the tea shop profits exceeding all my expectations, especially with the new extension upstairs, I'm investing some of my money in a house. It's inland, like Rory's, but it has a fantastic view of the nearby farmer's flower fields. I picture when I have my kitchen door open on warm days the scent of the flowers will waft in. A sheer delight while I'm cooking.'

'It sounds wonderful. And I bet you'll have a well–kitted kitchen.'

'The kitchen is one of those big old farmhouse types and I plan to do with it the same as I've done with the tea shop — combine vintage and modern styling. I'll be able to try out my new recipes there rather than working late here at the tea shop kitchen. I've ideas for lots of new cakes and scone recipes.'

'I'd love to be able to make a light and fluffy scone. Mine are okay, hit or miss. But I enjoy cooking.

Skye and I both cook, but I wish I could be a better baker.'

She wasn't hinting, but Lyle brightened and offered to give her a few tips.

'Want to bake some scones with me tonight? Unless you have to dash off home.'

Holly was in no hurry to leave. She was having a relaxing and fun time with Lyle.

'Are you sure I won't mess up your schedule? I know you have to bake scones and cakes ready for the tea shop.'

Lyle was up and bustling over to a cupboard to get her a clean apron. 'Tonight, you can be my assistant. I'll show you how to make perfect scones.'

Holly felt a rush of enthusiasm take her off guard, and accepted the apron with glee.

Lyle washed his hands and then gestured for her to do the same while he set up the ingredients.

'Use your fingertips to rub the butter into the flour,' he said, and then instructed each step of the scone recipe. 'Add a light sprinkling of flour to the rolled scone mix before using your cutter. Press firmly, don't wiggle the cutter around.'

She did as he instructed her. 'These look so much better than mine.' The delight sounded in her voice.

'I like to flip some of my scones over before I put them on the baking tray so the flat bottom is on top. I think it makes the scones rise more evenly.'

'I'll try that.'

Lyle had preheated the oven. 'Pop your scones in and time them.'

She checked the recipe he'd given her to follow. 'Timer set.' She grinned happily at him, enjoying an evening of baking. 'Any other tips on how I can be a better baker?'

'Practise is the key. Once you can rustle up a light sponge cake, well risen scones, and a traditional apple pie so you learn how to bake shortcrust pastry with a filling without having a soggy bottom—'

Holly giggled. 'Lyle's troubleshooting tips for baking.'

He laughed. 'You know what I mean,' he said, wagging a scolding finger at her. 'Learn the basics. That's when you can tackle most baking recipes with confidence. Actually learn and practise. Then you can apply that knowledge and experience when baking other things.'

'That makes sense. If I learned how to make a light sponge, it could be a Victoria sponge cake, or cupcakes and butterfly cakes. I could add dried fruit to my scones or treacle or grated cheese.'

Lyle nodded as she continued.

'And I get what you mean about baking an apple pie.' She nodded firmly. 'I'll learn and practise the basics — sponge cake, scones and pie. I find baking and cooking relaxing.' She flicked through the recipe book he'd given her. 'A recipe for custard...hmmm.'

'There's something comforting about homemade custard,' he said. 'It takes me back to when I was a wee boy and I'd have jam roly–poly with homemade custard for pudding. Or apple pie and custard.'

'You've sparked my interest.' She continued to look through the recipes.

'Take the book with you. It has all the basics.'

'Thanks, I'll get it back to you.' She tucked it in her bag. As she did this, she felt her opinion of Lyle change, realising she'd underestimated him. Lyle had done well for himself building up his tea shop. She knew some days she'd hardly noticed him when she'd popped in to buy cakes and scones.

'I'm sorry, Lyle,' she heard herself murmur.

'For what?'

She couldn't bring herself to tell him. It seemed insulting. 'For taking up your time,' she said, fudging the truth.

He rightly didn't see why she'd suddenly made such a comment. 'I've baked more scones than I'd planned this evening, thanks to your chatty company.'

'I talk too much.'

'No you don't.'

The oven pinged, rescuing her from continuing to downplay their time together.

He pulled the batch of scones out and sat them down. 'There you go. They're perfectly risen, nicely browned and smell scrumptious.'

Holly smiled as the conversation got back on track to the happy chatter between them.

'Now for the taste test.' He went over to the fridge and lifted out a pat of butter and cut two scones open. 'We should wait until they cool a wee bit, but we're in a daring mood tonight, aren't we?'

'We are,' she said firmly. 'Lashings of butter for me.'

Spreading the butter on the scones, watching it melt around the edges, he gestured for her to try one.

Holly lifted up half a scone and bit into the freshly baked treat. 'Oh, yes, sooo tasty. And this butter is delicious.'

'I make it myself.'

Holly leaned back and gave him a questioning look. 'You make your own butter? With a dairy churn?' She thought he was winding her up.

'No, just with a mixer. It's easy. When I'm busy baking batches of cakes and scones I use bought butter. However, when I've time, I make up a couple of pats of my own butter. It's easy to whip up double cream into a buttery consistency. I'll show you.'

Lyle proceeded to show Holly how to make butter. He whipped the double cream in a mixer until it separated. Then he drained off the excess liquid, squeezing it all out until he was left with the buttery mix. 'Season with salt if you want, but I prefer mine unsalted.'

Holly watched him create the butter, learning his techniques.

'Try a taste of it,' he offered.

Using a clean spoon she sampled it and nodded with enthusiasm. 'Oh, yes!'

He finally shaped the mixture on a piece of baking paper into a butter pat. He put it in a glass butter dish. 'Now we pop it in the fridge to set.'

'What do you do with the buttermilk you drained off?'

'I keep it in the fridge and use it for baking.'

The delight showed on her face as she learned that this was something she could do herself at home.

'Homemade butter! Wait until I tell Skye.'

By the time she'd helped him tidy up, the conversation had swung towards talking about the ball, and that Lyle had experience of catering for balls.

'What about the dancing? Was everyone waltzing around the ballroom? Is there anything I should know about or practise?'

'I never danced at one. I worked on the catering. But I remember before a particular event that they had someone instructing guests how to waltz while wearing a ball gown. Posture was important and feeling the movement of the ball gown to enhance the grandeur of sweeping around the floor.' He demonstrated taking someone in hold while making sure his posture was correct.

Holly shook her head. 'I'm concerned that I'll trip if I look up and gaze out as I dance around the room.'

'It's easy, come on,' he said, clasping her hand and leading her through to the front shop. He pulled two of the tables aside to clear a space to allow them to waltz around.

Holly went along, hoping to learn from Lyle.

'I don't need to remind a model like you to keep their posture upright. But let me show you what it's like in hold.'

She let him take her in his arms, correct both their posture so that she felt like someone from a bygone era dancing around the vintage tea shop.

'Head up, shoulders down, rest your hand gently on my shoulder and let me lead. You're trying to lead.'

'Sorry, you're right.' She corrected her stance and let Lyle lead them around the floor.

'Keep a steady beat, one two three, one two three...'

'It's hard to do without music.'

'One moment, Cinders, I can remedy that.' He ran over to the shop counter and turned on the background music he sometimes played. Traditional music, ideal for a makeshift waltz.

He ran back and took her in hold again. 'Where were we...'

Holly listened to the music and soon they were dancing smoothly, elegantly and easily around the tea shop.

She started giggling.

This set him off.

'Stop it. You're making me laugh,' she said.

'You started it, Madam.'

'Miss. I'm not married.'

'You ought to be. You're a beautiful and talented young lady.'

They were play acting, teasing, having fun, being silly.

And yet...Holly found herself again looking at Lyle with a fresh eye. He was a fine looking man, so sweet and cheerful, and willing to invite her into his world for a little while this evening. She didn't feel that he had any hidden agenda. There was nothing hidden behind his kind words and happy attitude.

'There you go,' he said as the song ended. 'You're ready to waltz the night away at the castle ball.'

She stepped back and brushed her auburn hair back from her lovely face. 'Thank you for making time for

133

me in your busy schedule, and showing me how to waltz with aplomb.'

'Any time.'

She felt that he meant this, and her heart squeezed as she gazed at him.

'Well, I'd better be off home now. Skye will still be causing mischief at the castle with Innis, but I have things to stitch, sort and mend for the shop.'

He fetched her coat and accessories from the kitchen.

She put them on, wrapping up well.

It was then he realised that Skye had the car.

'I'll give you a lift up to your house.'

'No, it's fine, I'll walk up the hill.'

Lyle grabbed his jacket and car keys. 'Nonsense. It's snowing. Come on.'

Locking the shop but leaving the lights on, he opened the car door for her and then ran round and jumped into the driver's seat.

It was a short drive to her house, the one she shared with Skye. Their parents were still away touring the mainland, islands and visiting relatives and friends.

He waited in the car while she ran in, clutching the bag of scones he'd insisted she take. 'You made them,' he'd told her.

Waving to him, Holly hurried inside and closed the door to one of the cheeriest evenings she'd had in a while.

Shrugging off her coat, she lit the fire in the lounge and then sat reading through the recipe book Lyle had given her, making a note of the ingredients, including flour, butter, eggs and double cream, that she planned to buy from the grocery shop in the morning to practise her new baking skills.

CHAPTER NINE

Skye helped Innis put the chocolates they'd made into boxes that he stored in the castle kitchen. She'd learned a few things from how to melt and mix the chocolate to decorating the truffles and bon bons.

Nairne had finished work for the night and they now had the kitchen to themselves.

'I know it's getting late, but can I offer you another cup of tea before you leave?' he said, not wanting their night to end.

'Yes, thanks.'

Innis was making the tea when Finlay walked in. Merrilees had already left after having dinner with Finlay and had driven back to stargazer cottage before the snow became any heavier.

'It's been a busy night, but the guests seem happy with the buffet menu,' said Finlay.

'I'll second that,' Skye added lightly.

'Ah, and there I was thinking you were only enticed here by Innis' chocolates,' Finlay joked with her. 'And Murdo has put aside two sledges for you and Holly.'

Skye looked to Innis for an explanation.

'I wanted to make sure two sledges were put in the storeroom for you,' Innis told her, explaining the details.

'Can I have a peek?' She was eager to see what she'd be using to beat him. 'It'll help me plan my winning tactics when I challenge you on the slopes.'

Finlay smiled and backed away. 'I'll leave you two to enjoy the rest of your date.'

'It's not a date,' Innis corrected him. Then he saw the disappointment on Skye's face. 'Sort of, but not quite...with potential.' He rambled.

Skye blinked, trying to hide her reaction.

Finlay gave an exaggerated response. '*Okay*...whatever this is, or isn't, I have to attend to the guests. Have fun, with potential.' Smirking to himself, he left them alone together and went back through to the function room.

'I didn't mean to embarrass you,' Innis insisted.

'You didn't,' she said. This was true.

'Or disappoint you,' he added.

'You really didn't,' she lied. With one comment he'd dashed her hopes, before making a spectacular effort to redress the issue. Where did that leave them? She wasn't sure.

'I'll get your coat from reception and show you the sledges, if you're still interested.'

'I am.'

Striding away, he left her for a couple of minutes to wander around the kitchen. Through the glass door she saw the snow was still falling quite heavily. Before she could decide whether to be sensible and head home now, Innis was back with her pink wool coat, hat and mittens.

Skye put them on and pulled up the collar of her coat.

Innis threw his jacket, changed his shoes for boots that he had in a cupboard, and opened the back door, letting the snowy air blow in.

Skye followed him as he led the way outside. The freezing cold was in such contrast to the heat of the kitchen that she felt it take her off guard. Pulling her hat down to cover her ears, she trudged through the snow, following Innis towards the back door of the storeroom.

Her boots disturbed the layer of snow that covered the entire patio.

She gazed at the trees that edged the nearby forest. Everything was covered with snow, and in the pale moonlight and glow from the castle, it sparkled like white icing sugar.

'It's beautiful, like a scene from a winter fairytale,' she commented, looking all around her. Large, fluffy flakes continued to flutter down from the night sky. She felt the icy snowflakes fall on her upturned face.

She was so engrossed in the scenery that she didn't notice the pot plants at the edge of the patio and almost tumbled over them.

Innis lunged at her, scooping her up, preventing her from falling. 'Careful there.' His rich voice sounded clear and sensual in the icy air.

'Clumsy me.' She righted herself and tried to calm her heart that reacted so intensely whenever Innis was near her.

It was her own fault for accepting his invitation to see his chocolate making, she chided herself. Now here she was in a real life romantic dilemma that had been part of her dreams for some time.

Innis pulled open the storeroom door and gestured for Skye to step inside. 'The sledges are in here.'

Skye stepped in, feeling the temperature rise, not just from the warmth of the room, but from the effect Innis had on her.

They were alone in the storeroom now. The castle was on wind down for the evening with most of the staff having gone home. The snow could be treacherous during its first fall, and they'd left promptly to head away from the castle before the landscape disappeared completely under a blanket of snow.

The two sledges were covered with a light tarpaulin to protect them during storage.

Innis whipped it off and was impressed with Murdo's handiwork. The sledges had been cleaned and polished and looked like new. They were quite modern, one pink, one turquoise. Murdo had replaced the cords with fresh ones.

The styling was sporty. From his experience of whizzing down the slopes on sledges since he was a boy, he was set to be pitted against all challengers. Murdo had put Innis' sledge aside along with ones for Finlay and Ean.

'Is there steering?' Skye bent down to study the pink sledge. Her name was written on a tag and tied to it. Holly's name was on the turquoise one.

'No, just sit in and hold on tight. Use your body to alter the angle and route you take as you whiz down the slopes.'

'You make it sound...daring.' There was no other word for it that sprang to mind.

'It is. You're the daring type though,' he told her.

'Me? Daring? No, not really. What makes you think that?'

'You're here with me, doing things you've never tried before. And yes, it did involve eating chocolate, but still...'

'Eating sweeties and swerving trees down a snowy incline...' She held her hands out, palms up as if weighing the difference between the two. Secretly there was a third option that was the most challenging and romantically dangerous of all — feeling herself falling for Innis. Now that could lead to a ton of trouble.

He saw the turmoil on her face, mistaking it for reluctance to compete against him. 'You can forgo the challenge, Skye. But what started as a joke could be quite...adventurous.' He withheld the words dangerous and foolhardy. And what on earth were they thinking challenging each other. Instead he smiled casually, hoping she didn't sense how much his heart longed to be with her.

'I'm up for adventure.' Her tone was decisive, leaving him in no doubt that he had a real challenger on his hands. One that could break his heart and cause more damage than any tumble from a sledge in the snow.

The time was wearing on and he led her back out of the storeroom into the snow. The flakes were falling heavier and he knew from experience that the roads would be getting trickier to drive on.

Not even thinking about this, Skye paused and gazed up at the snow falling all around them. 'This is wonderful.' She did an involuntary twirl, arms out, palms up to catch the snowflakes. 'It really feels like Christmas.'

He found himself torn between asking her to go with him to the ball, and being sensible and suggesting she should head home before the snow became even heavier. Once it had covered everything and settled overnight, the roads were more reliable, but tonight he wondered how to keep her safe on her drive down to the coast.

The latter won through and he heard the reluctance in his voice as he suggested they end their evening now.

'I'll drive ahead of you. Follow me, slow and steady, along the road,' he advised her.

'I can manage fine. I'll be careful. I don't want you having to drive down and then back again because of me.'

He'd have done it a few times without complaint. Just spending time with her was what he'd enjoyed more than anything at the moment.

'No, follow me,' he insisted in that tone she knew so well.

Leading her back into the kitchen, he picked up one of the boxes of chocolates on the way, and they headed through reception and out to where their cars were parked in front of the castle.

He helped her clear her windows of snow and then prepared his car.

With a wave, he got into his car and drove off, seeing her car headlights following him away from the castle and towards the forest road.

Skye glanced at the forest looking like someone had sprinkled it with icing sugar. It was beautiful and imposing in equal measures.

She kept the heater on and the window wipers continually brushed the snow from the windscreen as she watched Innis's car navigate the way down to the coast road.

The sea was strangely calm, barely a ripple, and with the flakes of snow tumbling down, it looked like it was frozen all the way out to the other islands. A rush of excitement washed over her. The evening with Innis had been everything she'd hoped for and more. He wanted to be romantic. He'd admitted that. And the word *potential* kept rewinding through her thoughts. Was there potential for romance with Innis? Not just a Christmas fling, but a deeper love than she could ever wish for.

Concentrate on the road, she scolded herself, feeling her thoughts drift.

The usual five minute drive took twice as long, but soon he was leading her up to the front of her house. The lights were on and a Christmas tree shone in the window.

Skye knew that Holly would be waiting up for her, keen to hear the gossip. And she had plenty to tell her. A late, late night was in the offing.

Innis got out of his car carrying the box of chocolates and handed them to her as he walked her up to her front door. Fairy lights were draped around the lintel and a lantern illuminated them both in its glow.

'Thank you for coming up to the castle tonight, Skye.'

'No, thank you for inviting me. I now have a better idea of your chocolatier work. And I appreciate the box of chocolates.'

He thought he smiled at her, but he wasn't sure because numerous conflicting thoughts were distracting him. Skye's soft, sweet lips were a distraction in themselves, and the way her trusting blue eyes looked up at him. Ask her, just ask her to go to the ball, he urged himself. And then immediately changed his mind. Their evening had been perfect. He didn't want to risk ruining it. He would ask her, but not just now. There was time to do it before the ball. He could pop into her dress shop in the morning and perhaps invite her then.

She was still looking at him, waiting, as he appeared to be wanting to say something.

'Goodnight, Skye,' he said in that deep voice that sent her heart racing.

'Goodnight.' She opened the door and stood there to wave him off, watching his car navigate the snowscape with proficient ease.

He couldn't get her out of his thoughts as he drove back to the castle. By the time he'd reached the forest he wished he'd invited her to go with him to the ball. He wrung out his frustration on the steering wheel and drove on towards the castle that was all aglow against the snowy sky.

Finlay was heading up the private staircase when Innis arrived. They walked up together.

'How did the rest of your evening go with Skye?' said Finlay. 'Any further progress with your potential?'

143

'I think so.'

They walked along the hallway that led to their suites. 'Did you ask her to go to the ball with you?'

'No.'

'Where's the potential in that?'

'I'm working up to it. I'm planning to talk to her tomorrow morning. I didn't want to ruin the nice evening we'd had.'

Finlay shook his head. 'Could be bad timing. Merrilees says the dress shop is due for a large delivery of ball gowns in the morning. You'll be in the middle of that.'

Innis wasn't put off. 'It'll give me a chance to show an interest in the ball gowns.'

Finlay gave him an incredulous look. 'You're interested in ball gown fashion?'

Innis sighed and paused outside his door. They stopped to continue their conversation. 'I'm trying to take an interest in the things that Skye is interested in.'

'That's great, but how are you going to get a private moment with her if she's up to her eyes in dresses? Unless you're just going to ask her on a date in front of others. Merrilees is going to the shop in the morning. They've earmarked a couple of dresses for her and she's keen to see them as soon as they arrive.'

'Point taken. But...I'll find a way to talk to her on her own sometime tomorrow.'

'You should, because according to the guest list of those already booked to attend the ball, there are a lot of couples. All it will take is one man to ask Skye to go with him to the ball and—'

'I'm going to do it,' Innis assured him, knowing that Finlay only wanted him to be happy.

They bid each other goodnight, and then Innis mentioned Ean. 'Where's Ean? I haven't seen him tonight.'

Finlay paused and glanced back. 'He was out in the snow taking photos so he can paint snowscapes. He showed me some of the pictures and they're really incredible. I'm going to put some of them up on the website to advertise the castle. And speaking of advertising, the feature that Merrilees wrote is out in tomorrow's newspaper. I've asked Murdo to buy extra copies for us.'

'I'll buy one for my shop.'

Having agreed on their plans, they both headed into their private suites to get some sleep. It was another early start in the morning. And now with the snow to contend with people being caught off guard because it started early, they knew the day was going to be extra hectic.

'You were baking scones with Lyle all evening and dancing in his tea shop?' The incredulous tone of Skye's voice was clear.

Holly smiled and popped a chocolate in her mouth.

They sat having tea and a few of the chocolates by the fire, exchanging their latest news.

Holly shrugged and enjoyed the rich chocolate truffle.

'Spill, I want all the details,' Skye insisted, curling up on her fireside chair ready to hear every detail.

Holly took a sip of her tea. 'Nothing happened. We baked, we danced. We had fun.'

'That's a whole lot of nothing.'

Holly giggled.

'Start from the beginning,' said Skye. 'Lyle invited you to have dinner with him at the tea shop.'

'A bowl of soup and bread. He was cooking it for his dinner and I mentioned that we'd been too busy getting ready for the carol singing to have dinner.'

'Was he trying to chat you up?'

'Nooo, not at all. That's what made me look at him in a different light. To actually notice that he's nice, and fun, and very talented with his baking. I told him I'd love to bake better scones and he offered to teach me. He was baking them anyway, so I stayed. With you being at the castle, I thought...why not?'

'So Lyle is becoming an acquired taste after all.' There was a knowing smile in Skye's voice.

'Maybe. Maybe we'll keep things as just friends. But he's quite fit, and a fine looking man. And we get along. He was so easy to talk to, and I got the feeling that he wasn't pretending to be interested in what I was chatting about — dresses, fashion, more dresses. We discussed fabric. He selected the yellow gingham for his tea shop kitchen curtains.'

Skye's heart felt a warmth, seeing that Holly had enjoyed her evening with Lyle.

'And he let me borrow one of his recipe books.' She had the book tucked beside her and held it up. 'Do you want to try a scone I baked using one of the recipes? They're in a bag in the kitchen.'

Skye stood up. 'I'll make more tea. You butter the scones.'

'What about you and Innis?' Holly said as they made their late night snack. 'Any progress on the romance front?'

'Sort of. He admitted that he wants to be more romantic.' Skye explained the details of her conversation with Innis.

'Was he?'

'It's hard to tell with Innis, but I'd say he's working up to it.'

'Progress.'

'With *potential*.' Skye revealed what he'd said to Finlay.

They carried their tea and scones through to the fire and sat down, still exchanging gossip and giggles.

CHAPTER TEN

Snow continued to fall overnight, but had stopped by the morning. The main street shone under the bright winter sunlight, and everything from the shops to the hills rising up from the shore looked like they were encrusted with diamonds against a blanket of white snow.

The Christmas market stalls were set up regardless of the surprise snowfall, and everyone was bustling around getting ready to sell their crafts and other produce. The stalls were arranged in a niche near the town's Christmas tree, handy for shoppers. Ailsa had made an early start and her craft stall was ready for customers looking for craft gifts. This included her handmade jewellery and tiara hair bands that she hoped would interest those attending the ball.

Rowen's knitting stall had a selection of her latest range of yarns, and she'd made items like woolly hats, shawls and tea cosies to advertise the yarn and these were for sale too.

Snowflakes had settled around the edges of Innis' cake shop, creating a picture–perfect look to the cakes on display in the front window.

Roofs and roads were blue–white where the sunlight beams shone down from the cloudless blue winter sky.

Everything dazzled, bedecked in white, with the colourful shops adding pops of pastel pinks, yellows and blues to the picturesque scene.

The tide was out, and all along the coast the sand was a whiteout of snow, and the silvery–blue sea kept its calm during the beautiful December morning.

Finlay had taken his yacht that was anchored in the harbour for a trip around the island. He'd taken Merrilees with him. She was wrapped up in a light cream jacket and matching woolly hat.

The aquamarine hull cut through the sea, and the white sails billowed in the breeze, emphasising the yacht's ability to challenge the winter sea and Finlay's skills as an accomplished yachtsman.

Standing at the helm, he wore a stylish white, crew neck sailing jacket, and the wind blew through his thick blond hair. Finlay was in his element, and even more so these days now that he could share his world with Merrilees.

The advertising feature about the fairytale ball at the castle was out in the daily newspaper. Finlay had bought a couple of copies from the grocery shop before they boarded the yacht. A flick through the pages confirmed that it had been included as planned, but now it was tucked away below deck to be read thoroughly after they'd had their morning sail.

Sailing around the island after the first snow fall of winter was a tradition Finlay had created for himself. He enjoyed it all the more seeing Merrilees smile and squeal with delight as he sailed at speed using the expensive yacht's sleek design to full advantage. He'd won trophies in various sailing challenges and she knew he was well capable of handling the yacht. Nevertheless, feeling the yacht slice through the icy water at a fast rate of knots was invigorating.

After a lap around the island, he planned to anchor back at the harbour so Merrilees could go to the vintage dress shop to see the ball gowns.

The first delivery of ball gowns had arrived and Skye and Holly were busy unpacking each exquisite dress, gasping at the gorgeous fabrics, from tulle to taffeta and voile to velvet. The colours ranged from white and pale lemon to pastel pink, hues of blue, and lilacs that deepened to heliotrope, purple, red and burgundy.

The rails in the shop were festooned with fabulous ball gowns. Most had been worn once, to a special party, dance or ball, the wearer unknown, the event a mystery, but the beauty of each dress showed that someone in the past had loved it. Every pre–loved ball gown was hung carefully on the rails they'd had ready for the new arrivals. And soon the customers seeking a dress for the ball would love each design once again.

'The pink ball gown is here!' Skye couldn't contain her excitement as she unpacked the dress and held it up in front of her to admire it in the dressing room mirror.

'It's perfect for you,' said Holly.

'It is, isn't it.' The pale pink organza sparkled under the lights, and the fitted bodice and full skirt looked like they would need little, if any, alteration.

'Try it on before everyone starts popping in to see the new dresses,' Holly encouraged her.

Needing no encouragement at all, Skye put the dress on and smiled when she saw how beautifully the bodice encrusted with sequins and crystals flattered her slender curves, and then the layers of organza

150

sprinkled with sparkle sat out into full ball gown splendour.

'With heels on, it'll be the ideal length so I won't even have to alter the hem.'

Every now and then, a vintage dress that looked like it was designed for either Skye or Holly, made its way to their shop. Sometimes it was a tea dress, a tartan wrap, a little cocktail number from the thirties, a retro chambray sundress, or a classic evening dress.

They both had favourites hanging in their wardrobes at home or in the shop but not for sale. At the back of the shop they had two rails of dresses that they called *currently loved*. These were owned and loved by them. Perhaps one day they'd sell them as *pre–loved* for someone else to enjoy, but their little collection of cherry picked chic was their personal fashion favourites.

Adding ball gowns to this collection wasn't practical, but practicality wasn't a consideration when it came to dressing like a fairytale princess. Skye pictured the sparkling pink dress as part of her *currently loved* fashions.

Lyle bagged two Scottish fern cakes, stuck a *back in five minutes* sign on the front window of his tea shop, put his sunglasses on, and hurried along to the vintage dress shop.

Innis saw him go by and wondered why he was wearing sunglasses. The snow wasn't bright enough to merit shades, and there was something in Lyle's manner that reeked of mischief.

151

He peered out the cake shop window to see where Lyle was headed. The dress shop. Yes, he was up to something. But what?

Innis had been steeped in his own thoughts, replaying the ideal scenario whereby he walked into the dress shop and if Holly was there, which was likely, and a customer viewing the ball gowns, he'd take Skye aside for a private moment. Perhaps they'd go into the kitchen. So far, so good. Then he'd tell her how much he enjoyed her company at the castle making chocolates, and finally ask her to go with him to the ball.

The dress shop was buzzing with women eager to see the latest ball gowns. The grocery shop had already sparked the local gossip about the newspaper feature, and this had added to the interest in buying a dress for the ball.

Undeterred by the buzz, Lyle made an entrance wearing the sunglasses and a bright smile. 'Morning, ladies.'

Unfazed by the arrival of Lyle, the customers giggled but continued to rummage through the rails.

'I knew you'd be too busy this morning to pop to my tea shop, so...here you go. Special delivery.' Lyle put the bag of fern cakes on the counter.

Skye peeked in the bag. 'Oh, tasty, thank you.'

'Is there a reason for the sunglasses?' Holly said to him.

'You said that you were due a delivery of dazzling dresses, sparkle and sequins galore,' he explained. 'So I thought I'd better wear these.'

Holly and Skye laughed, and so did the customers.

152

'Anyway, I'd better scoot back to my tea shop.' He went to leave, but Skye had a couple of questions for him.

'Holly says you have ball dance experience,' said Skye. 'You showed her how to waltz last night, but when she was trying to show me, we couldn't get the stance right.'

'You said something about resting a couple of fingertips on your shoulders or was it tilting the hand?' Holly chimed in. 'I was going to look at videos online, but as you're here...could you show us?'

Always willing to help, he nodded cheerfully and had just taken Skye in hold when Innis walked in.

'If we were dancing around the floor at the ball—' Lyle stopped instructing Skye, suddenly noticing the tall figure standing glaring at him.

Mistakenly thinking that Lyle was making a play for Skye, Innis thought the warnings he'd had were true. Another man would step in and ask Skye to the ball. The pang of longing he felt for her caused him to override all hesitation. He needed to do something now. Right now, because there was Lyle, trying to look cool in his sunglasses, showing Skye how they'd dance around the floor!

'*Innis...*'

Amid the adrenalin pumping through his system, Innis heard Skye utter his name.

But instead of responding, he forged ahead boldly.

'Skye,' Innis announced in his rich, deep voice. 'Will you go with me to the ball?'

The buzz in the shop became silent and everyone stared at Innis.

Skye gulped. Did Innis just ask her in front of everyone? She'd thought he'd been holding back, waiting for the right moment to ask her. With her mind in a whirl, she hesitated longer than she'd intended before replying.

Innis thought his heart thundering in his chest was loud enough for everyone to hear. He stood there, hoping Skye would accept, but her hesitation tore through him.

'Yes, I'd love to go with you to the ball, Innis.' Skye forced what she hoped was a relaxed smile, trying to hide the fact that her stomach was doing back–flips.

Innis nodded and wasn't sure if he smiled. 'Thank you for accepting my proposal.'

A group intake of breath charged through the shop.

'Not a marriage proposal,' Innis stumbled to clarify. And then he scolded himself. You sound like a total fool.

'Right, I have to scuttle back to my tea shop,' Lyle said, wanting to escape the pressure cooker atmosphere.

With a cheery wave, Lyle was gone.

'I have to get back to my cake shop too.' The tone of Innis' voice resonated deep and strong.

Skye's wide blue eyes gazed at Innis in wonderment.

Nodding at Skye, and then at the others, as if it was some sort of formal address, Innis strode out of the dress shop leaving behind him an impression that Skye, Holly and the others would never forget.

'Did Innis just almost ask you to marry him?' Elspeth said to Skye. She'd left Morven to watch the knitting shop while she went to see the dresses.

'No,' said Skye. Turmoil and elation battled to take charge of her tone. Innis hadn't proposed, but was this remotely in his mind? Had he blurted out a hidden intention?

Nettie was there and spoke up. 'It's clear that he wants to.'

A blush started to rise in Skye's cheeks.

'Did he think that Lyle was making a play for you?' Holly wondered.

'I'm not sure.' The only thing Skye was sure of was that she had a date with Innis to go to the ball.

Innis walked into the cake shop and through to the kitchen to get on with his baking. Rosabel and Primrose were serving customers, but from their relaxed manner they hadn't yet heard the gossip about his invitation to Skye.

Melting chocolate to make ganache for pouring over a chocolate cake, he had a bet on with himself. He gave it fifteen minutes before the gossip filtered through to them.

Squeals of surprise sounded from Rosabel and Primrose in the front shop.

Make that five minutes, he recalculated.

Keeping his head down and melting the smooth ganache, he was aware of two smiling, eager faces peering in the kitchen at him.

'Say it and be done with it,' he said without taking his eyes off the ganache.

The giggling said it all.

Holly had messaged them with the news. No surprises there.

As customers came into the shop, Rosabel and Primrose went back through to serve them, while chattering about the happy news.

Finlay lifted Merrilees from the deck of the yacht on to the harbour's edge. She could've managed to step off fine by herself, but he playfully lifted her, holding her in his arms for a moment and smiling at her.

Her laughter rang clear in the cold air.

'Have fun ball gown buying,' Finlay said, gave her a kiss, and then drove off to the castle, leaving Merrilees to go into the dress shop with a heart full of anticipation. Holly and Skye had promised to earmark dresses for her and she couldn't wait to see what they'd selected.

The shop was busy and Merrilees saw Rory wave in the window to grab Skye and Holly's attention as she entered the shop.

Skye stepped outside for a moment. 'What can I do for you, Rory?'

'Rowen is working at her market stall this morning, but she's planning to pop in to buy a dress for the ball later. Whatever she buys, I want to pay for it,' he insisted.

Skye smiled at him. 'That's very romantic of you.'

Rory shrugged. 'I just want to treat her to something nice.'

'I'll make sure she gets a lovely dress,' Skye assured him.

Happy that he'd done this, Rory waved and headed into the cake shop.

'Can I talk to Innis?' Rory said to Primrose.

'Yes, he's in the kitchen, away through.'

He wore his jeans, a chunky Aran jumper and a denim jacket with a warm lining.

Innis looked up as Rory bounded in and pulled a folded envelope of plans from his jacket pocket.

'I've drawn up the building plans for your extension, all nice and neat. This is a copy for you. Peruse it at your leisure and let me know if you want any alterations.' Rory put the envelope down on the kitchen table, not expecting to stay. He'd just popped in to drop off the plans.

Innis wiped any residue of cocoa powder off his hands and opened up the plans, nodding firmly when he saw them. 'First class. I'll have a proper look later, but this is excellent.'

Rory grinned. He'd made a thorough job of designing the extension for the cake shop. He pointed to the windows. 'These will be double glazed, but this section here can open out in the summer on to the garden.'

'It's great.' Innis was pleased, but the backlash of what he'd done in the dress shop gnawed at him. He thought he hid it well.

'Did someone steal your sweeties?' Rory said bluntly.

For one moment Innis thought to hide what was wrong, but decided against it and told Rory what had happened in the dress shop.

Rory rocked back on the heels of his sturdy boots. 'I've just been in the dress shop. It's jumping this morning. I couldn't even get in.' He explained about buying Rowen a dress. 'And you asked Skye in front of all those customers?'

'I hadn't planned to. I wanted to talk to her in private. But when I went in, Lyle was there, all cool looking in his sunglasses, showing Skye how to dance at the ball—'

Rory cut–in. 'Hang on, Lyle was wearing sunglasses? It's winter. It's snowing. What was he thinking?'

'I think he was making a move on Skye. So I jumped in and asked her before he could do it.'

Rory frowned. 'Why would Lyle do that when he spent last night having dinner with Holly in his tea shop, showing her how to bake scones.'

This was news to Innis. 'Lyle was with Holly last night in his tea shop?'

'Yes, they had a fun time. While you and Skye were making chocolates up at the castle, Lyle was baking and boogying with Holly. They were waltzing around his tea shop. No romance. But I think there's potential for it.'

'Are you in a hurry?' Innis said to him.

'No...'

'Pour yourself a cup of tea, grab a cake, any cake, and sit down for a minute. Are you sure that's what happened with Lyle and Holly?'

Rory poured a mug of tea, lifted a cupcake and sat down to reveal everything that Lyle had told him earlier that morning when he'd been in the tea shop.

158

He often stopped by and wanted to check that everything was working after all the snow they'd had.

Innis shook his head and sighed heavily.

'Ach, don't fuss over that. We all make fools of ourselves sometimes over the lassies.'

Innis almost smiled. This was true. He'd made a fool of himself several times recently over Skye.

'Lyle wasn't making a pass at Skye, but you can be sure that some lad would, so now you're taking her to the ball. Isn't that what you wanted?'

It was. Innis nodded.

'The gossip would've sparked anyway whether you'd blown your trumpet about your feelings for Skye in front of a lot of folk or in private,' Rory reasoned.

'Yes, that's true. Thanks for taking the time to tell me about Lyle. He's been generous with his time and knowledge about our plans for the ball. I don't want any ructions.'

'I'll smooth things over with him if you want,' Rory offered.

'No, I'll tell him myself.'

Rory bit into his cake and drank his tea.

'I suppose we do all make fools of ourselves when it comes to romance,' Innis said thoughtfully.

Rory laughed. 'I saw Finlay twirling Merrilees around like a baton down at the harbour when he helped her off his yacht.'

They shared a smile.

Drinking down the remainder of his tea, Rory stood up. 'I'll let you get on with your baking.'

'Thanks again,' Innis said as Rory headed out.

'I'm stealing one of your chocolates,' Rory told him, grabbing a truffle from the confectionary display as he left the shop.

Innis laughed.

Rosabel and Primrose came hurrying through to the kitchen. 'Everything hunky–dory now?'

'Yes, Rory brought my plans for the extension.' He gestured to the architectural drawings on the table.

'Are we allowed a peek?' said Primrose.

'Yes.' Innis poured the ganache over the chocolate cake and started to smooth it over the surface. The melted chocolate mix ran down the edges and he used a spatula to create a glossy chocolate surface.

Primrose and Rosabel were eager to see the plans and nodded as they approved of the design.

'It's going to be a bright but cosy wee hub for serving tea and cakes,' Primrose commented.

'I like that it looks out on to the garden,' said Rosabel. 'It'll be lovely in the summer, but even on a snowy day like this, it'll be quite magical.'

Leaving the plans on the kitchen table, they hurried back through to serve customers.

A message pinged on Innis's phone. It was from Finlay.

Congratulations! I heard you asked Skye to go to the ball.

Yes. And I heard you twirled Merrilees around after you went sailing.

Gossip travels fast.

Too fast.

Have you seen the feature in the newspaper?

No, I'll pop out for a copy.

160

We've had a few bookings for the ball already because of it. Ean thinks we'll need more ice cream.

I agree. I'll talk to Brodrick.

Cheers.

Innis tucked his phone in his pocket. 'I won't be long. The castle's feature is in the paper. I'm popping to the grocery shop to buy a copy.'

'Buy one for us while you're there please,' Rosabel called after him as he headed out.

Innis raised his hand in acknowledgement and strode up the snowy street in his short shirt sleeves to buy the copies. He didn't feel the cold, only the warmth in his heart for Skye as the realisation sank in that she'd agreed to be his date for the ball.

CHAPTER ELEVEN

Armed with copies of the newspaper, Innis headed to the cafe bar to talk to Brodrick.

'We'd like to order extra ice cream for the buffet,' Innis told him.

'No problem,' said Brodrick as he worked behind the bar making coffee and hot chocolate for customers. 'I'll talk to Nairne for the exact quantities and flavours you need.'

'Great, I appreciate it. The advertising feature is out in the newspaper and Finlay says we've had people booking tickets for the ball because of it.'

'I'll phone Nairne and get the increased order sorted out. And I've tried some of those chocolate samples you gave me, and they work a treat in the ice cream, so I'll include those.'

'Do that.' He turned to leave but Brodrick's comment made him stop.

'Elspeth says you've asked Skye to go with your as your date for the ball. It's about time you two got together.'

Innis smiled and shook his head. 'Skye's challenged me to a sledging race the day before the ball.'

'Sorry, Innis, but my money is on Skye winning.'

'When it comes to Skye nothing would surprise me.'

Smiling, Innis left to tackle his next chore, smoothing things over with Lyle.

'Try one of my new festive yum yums.' Lyle thrust a plate piled with several of the iced treats at Innis as he walked up to the tea shop counter. Customers were sitting at tables enjoying tea, cake and scones, and the fire added warmth to the atmosphere.

'Is it a new recipe?' Innis picked one up and studied it, glad that Lyle didn't seem miffed regarding their earlier encounter.

'Yes, I've added a sprinkling of cinnamon and other spices that I use in my Christmas cakes.'

Innis took a bite and nodded. 'Very tasty,' he mumbled. 'I just wanted to say that I got the wrong end of the stick in the dress shop. I thought you were chatting up Skye.'

'Nooo.'

'I know that now. And I hear you had a cosy night with Holly.' He took another bite of his yum yum, waiting to hear the details.

'We're just friends. I was showing her how to bake scones.'

Innis gave him a knowing look. 'I heard you were waltzing her around the tea shop late at night.'

Lyle couldn't contain his smile. 'Nothing happened. It was all just friendly.'

Innis shrugged, smiled and then headed out eating the rest of his tasty treat.

The Christmas market was abuzz with activity and it was usual practise for Innis to buy items in support of the stallholders. He walked over to Ailsa's stall and she smiled when she saw him.

He admired the selection of fashion jewellery that glittered in the sunlight. It was almost lunchtime, and the snow had held off all morning.

'Looking for something in particular?' said Ailsa. 'Something for Skye?'

Innis grinned. 'Okay, what do you recommend?' Then he noticed the head bands. 'Are those tiaras?'

'Yes, but Skye has one already to match her pink ball gown. But what about a little evening bag.' Ailsa lifted a pink satin bag she'd decorated with pink sequins and crystals. 'It would be a fine match for her dress.'

'I'll take it, thanks. And I'll buy one of the pink gift bags you make.' He paid for the items, and then looked at the yarn in the next stall.

Rowen had sample bags of yarn made up from her latest ranges. 'These are my new yarns. There's enough in each bag to make a hat, mittens or something like that.' The bags were made up by colour.

'I'll take two bags of the pink yarn. One yellow, and one blue.' A pink and a yellow for Rosabel and Primrose. Pink for Skye and blue for Holly.

'Thanks, Innis,' Rowen said, handing him the four bags of yarn. She wanted to comment on his date with Skye, but kept her comments to herself.

Innis walked back to the cake shop loaded with the newspapers, the evening bag and the yarn.

'I bought these from Rowen's stall.' He gave a bag of pink yarn to Rosabel and the yellow yarn to Primrose.

They were delighted by the unexpected gifts of yarn.

'Thank you, Innis,' said Rosabel. 'This pink yarn is gorgeous.'

'Yes, I love the yellow,' Primrose added. 'That was very thoughtful of you.'

Innis walked on through to the kitchen leaving them to chatter about what they planned to knit with the yarn.

He put the evening bag down on a shelf out of harm's way. Ailsa had wrapped it up. Then he sat down for a moment to read the feature in the newspaper, nodding to himself as he noticed that Merrilees had mentioned everything from the castle being like something out of a fairytale, to the ballroom size function room, the hotel–style accommodation for guests, and that there would be a sumptuous buffet for the ball on Christmas Eve.

When he finished reading it, he sat back and phoned Finlay.

'I've just read the feature. Merrilees has done a great job. Even I want to go to the ball now.'

Finlay laughed. 'You'd better be there...with Skye.'

'Does everyone know?'

'Oh, yes. Including Ean. He's pleased for you. Now we've all got a date for the ball.'

Innis told him about talking to Lyle and Brodrick, bringing him up to date with everything.

'Thank Merrilees for doing such a great job with the feature,' Innis concluded.

'I'll do that.'

After the call, Innis got to work making his cakes and icing them. He was behind schedule and put a spurt on. By the afternoon he'd caught up with everything and then continued to work as the sky outside changed from bright blue to winter grey. The snow was on its way again. Another snowy night.

Skye continued to alter the ball gowns that had been bought earlier in the day. Thankfully, the alterations were minor, requiring mainly hems to be altered.

Although they'd tried to insist to the customers that they liked to check each dress and mend any wear and tear before selling it, quite a few of the ladies were members of the knitting bee and wanted to buy the ball gowns and take them away to sort themselves. As most of them were experienced in dressmaking and sewing, this made sense. The rails that had been full of ball gowns were now a little bit sparse, but the second half of the order was due to be delivered the next day. And Skye now had more time to work on making some of the evening dresses fit for the ball.

Holly hurried in carrying two lanterns. 'Sorry, I got held up. The stalls were busy, but I bought two lanterns.' She held them up. 'Aren't they lovely.'

'Yes, I'm looking forward to the lantern walk.'

Holly spoke in a confiding tone. 'Everyone was talking to me about you and Innis going to the ball.'

Skye blushed. 'I still can't believe he asked me in front of the entire shop.'

'He's apologised to Lyle. I happened to walk past the tea shop and popped in to see Lyle. I told him I'm going to practise making scones at home this evening.'

Holly told her what had happened between Lyle and Innis. 'So everything is fine. Oh, and...Rowen says Innis bought a load of yarn from her stall. Four bags full.'

Skye frowned. 'Innis doesn't knit.'

'I'm just saying.' Holly went through to the kitchen to make tea. 'We haven't stopped for lunch, but Lyle gave me a crusty baguette filled with cheese and salad. I was going to buy two small rolls, but Lyle said he wanted to give me a long one.' She filled the kettle. 'I thought we could have that and then get on with the dress alterations.'

'Great, I'll finish this hem and then we'll take a short break.'

They sat in the kitchen and ate their late lunch.

'I'm not supposed to tell you, but Ailsa says Innis bought a wee something for you from her stall,' Holly revealed.

'What did he buy me?'

'She wouldn't tell me. I think she thought I'd blab.'

Skye pondered what it could be.

After lunch, Skye and Holly ramped up their repairing for wearing methods, working on the ball gowns at speed to cut through the workload.

Holly draped a pale blue ball gown on to a mannequin in the front window and laughed when she glanced round at Skye working industriously at her sewing machine.

'You look like you're drowning in organza and sparkle.'

167

Skye pretended to swim to the surface and gurgled, gasping for air.

They were still laughing when Holly saw Innis loading white cardboard boxes into the back of his car. This was usual. They were delivered to the cake shop and then he took them up to the castle for his chocolatier work.

Holly waved out to him, not expecting him to gesture that he had something for them. At least that's what she interpreted the hand gestures as.

'Go to red alert! I think Innis is heading this way,' Holly warned Skye lightly.

Beeping and pretending to switch to red alert mode, Skye frantically tidied the wispy strands of hair that had escaped from her pinned up pleats.

'The wolf has wool!' Holly managed to tell Skye playfully before Innis arrived with the two bags of pink and blue yarn.

Innis walked in carrying the two bags full of yarn. 'I bought these from Rowen's stall at the Christmas market. I hope you can use them.' He wasn't sure where to put them down because almost every handy surface was covered with trays of sequins, crystals and fabric.

Skye unravelled herself from the dress she was sewing and accepted the bags. 'This pink yarn is so pretty.'

'I think you like pink,' he said. 'And you mentioned that you were knitting a red jumper so I thought this would be different.' He really didn't know what he was talking about but Skye seemed happy with the yarn.

Holly was pleased with the blue. 'Thank you, Innis. Rowen's yarn is lovely to knit with.'

'I think I'll knit a woolly hat to match my sledge,' Skye said with a mischievous grin. 'Dress for success. And you'll be able to see me easier in my pink hat as I race ahead of you.'

Innis smiled, shook his head and headed out. 'I'll leave you to get on with your sewing.'

They waved him off as he went back to his cake shop.

Admiring the yarn and planning what to knit with it, Skye finished sewing more sequins on to one of the ball gown bodices.

'Do you want to keep working here rather than head home?' said Holly. 'By the time we pack up all these sequins and stuff, and then set it all up at home after cooking dinner, we'd be as well continuing here. I'm sure I saw a couple of tins of soup in the kitchen cupboard.' Holly went through to check. 'Yes, but we really need to restock the cupboards.'

'I meant to buy a selection from the grocery shop, but it's been such a hectic time.'

Holly stood in the doorway of the kitchen and held up the two tins of soup. 'Lentil or broth?'

Skye had noticed people going by their shop and heading into Brodrick's cafe bar next door. 'We could pop out for a bite to eat. Less hassle, less to clear up.'

Holly thought this was a sensible idea.

'It's one of Brodrick's Christmas nights. I'll see how busy it is.'

Running out into the snowy night, Skye shivered as she peered in the window of the cafe bar. It was jumping with people. They'd never get a table.

'Hungry or practising being stealthy?' Innis' deep voice made her jump and turn around.

'Yes.'

As Innis grinned at her retort, Lyle approached.

'Is something sneaky going on? I saw you spying in the window of the cafe bar,' Lyle commented.

'Holly and I are working late at the shop and thought we'd grab something to eat at the cafe bar.' Skye glanced in the window. 'But it's jumping with people.'

By now Holly stood in the dress shop doorway joining in.

Lyle thumbed towards his tea shop. 'Come and have dinner with me. I've been batch baking quiche for my traditional festive tea event. I can spare one large quiche with salad trimmings and a pot of tea between the four of us.'

Innis reeled back. 'I wasn't planning to—'

'Come on,' Lyle encouraged them, walking away and waving them to follow him. 'We'll all freeze out here.'

Holly pulled the dress shop door shut and locked it.

And the four of them headed into the warmth of the tea shop.

'Make yourselves cosy by the fire,' Lyle called through to them as he marched ahead into the kitchen.

'I'll give you a hand,' Holly offered, following him, and leaving Skye and Innis to get a heat by the fire. Christmas lights pinned around the mantelpiece added to the cosy glow.

'Lyle has got a great business here,' Innis remarked. 'His hard work and talent for baking has paid off.'

'We had one of his savoury baguettes for lunch. If he keeps feeding us tasty treats, we'd be as well moving into the tea shop with him,' Skye joked.

'Ah, don't tempt me,' Lyle said, coming through with a tray of napkins, cutlery and condiments and setting them down on the table at the fire. 'Holly would train up well as my baking assistant extraordinaire. Though I doubt I'd be adept at dressmaking.'

Lyle hurried back to the kitchen as the oven pinged. 'The quiche is ready.'

Pulling a large quiche from the oven, he cut it into four generous wedges and put each slice on the four plates that Holly had set up.

'You're learning fast,' Lyle complimented her playfully.

'I have a top–level patisserie chef training me.'

Lyle laughed, and added side salads to the quiche, then carried two plates through while Holly grabbed the others.

'Is this your special quiche?' Innis recognised it from the pictures attached to the recipe he'd recommended to Nairne.

'It is. I've added extra courgette and cherry tomatoes, roast red onion, greentails and my own festive mix of spices,' said Lyle.

171

By now, Holly had brought the pot of tea and cups through on a tray.

Lyle poured the tea and sat down to enjoy dinner with his friends. He raised his tea cup and proposed at toast. 'To cosy nights and great company.'

The foursome tipped their cups together and then tucked into the quiche and salad.

'I'm certainly encouraging Nairne to include this on the ball's buffet menu,' said Innis.

'I hope you're serving this at your festive tea event,' Skye said, enjoying the savoury treat.

'I am indeed,' Lyle confirmed. 'And I've booked your table for two at one of the front windows upstairs in the new extension. The view of the sea is wonderful.'

'Thanks, Lyle,' Holly told him.

The warmth of the smile between them showed a spark of connection. Skye noticed and glanced at Innis. He'd noticed it too. They didn't say anything, but it was clear that the potential for a new romance was brewing between Holly and Lyle.

Christmas songs played unobtrusively in the background as they ate their meal and chatted about their business and plans for the festive season.

'I love this song,' said Holly. It had long been a favourite of hers.

Lyle stood up and held out his hand. 'May I have this dance before you run off to get on with your dressmaking?'

Giggling, Holly took his hand and he led her into the same space they'd danced the night before.

Skye smiled warmly for a moment, pleased that Holly had found romance for Christmas. It hadn't been a mystery man, but instead was the man she'd known all along.

'Shall we?' Innis' voice cut into her faraway thoughts.

'Yes.' Skye stood up and soon she was being held in his strong and capable hands, waltzing along with Holly and Lyle to the music while the snow fell outside the windows of the tea shop.

CHAPTER TWELVE

Snow was falling fast as Skye and Holly hurried back to the vintage dress shop. Innis accompanied them, doing his utmost to shield them from the cold. They'd thanked Lyle for dinner at the tea shop, enjoyed dancing to the Christmas songs, but then they needed to get back to the dress shop to get on with the dress alterations.

Holly unlocked the door and scurried inside, shaking the snow from herself.

Innis clasped hold of Skye's hand for a moment before she hurried in. His tall stature protected her from the full force of the snow and the wind sweeping in from the sea.

'I never intended asking you to go with me to the ball in front of everyone in the shop.' There was an apologetic tone in his voice, and his amber eyes gazed down at her.

'I know, it's fine,' Skye assured him. And for a brief moment she thought he was going to kiss her goodnight, but he pulled back and nodded in that way she'd become accustomed to.

Skye stepped inside the shop and closed the door against the snowy night. She peered through the flakes fluttering down, watching Innis get into his car and drive off home to the castle. It had been a day she'd never forget, and a night to remember.

Holly put the kettle on to make them a hot cup of tea while Skye set up her sewing machine to continue the dress alterations.

They chatted about their evening and the work they had to do while the kettle boiled.

Holly gazed out the window. 'Look at the snow falling into the sea. It looks magical.'

Skye looked round and viewed the scene. 'It's wild and so beautiful.'

'It is.' Holly sighed. 'I love living on the island. I don't miss the mainland at all.'

'Neither do I,' Skye agreed.

The kettle clicked off and Holly made the tea in the kitchen.

'Lyle seems very taken with you,' Skye called through to her.

'You think so?'

'Has he invited you to go with him to the ball?'

'No. We're still keeping things on a friendly note.'

Holly carried the tea through.

'Have you decided what ball gown you'd like to wear?'

'Not yet. I thought I'd wait until I see the next delivery. It should arrive in the morning.' She pulled up the list of dresses on her laptop on the counter. 'I saw this amber creation. I don't think the photo does it justice.'

Skye leaned over and viewed the dress. 'Amber satin overlaid with layers of light amber chiffon that's sprinkled with bronze and gold sparkles. It sounds gorgeous. But you're right, the photo doesn't show it properly.'

'The emerald velvet and organza is lovely too.'

'There are so many pretty dresses.'

Skye turned her attention back to the sewing. 'And so many to mend. I'm sure I'll dream about sequins in my sleep tonight.'

Holly laughed. 'And Innis.'

'I could say the same about you and Lyle.'

Holly didn't deny it as she unpicked the darts in the bodice of a dress that Nettie wanted to alter the fit. Then she planned to embroider strands of gold metallic thread over the stitch marks where the darts had been to disguise they'd ever been there.

'There's a feeling in the air this Christmas,' said Skye as she stitched sequins and crystals on to the bodice of her pink ball gown. 'And not just because of the fairytale ball at the castle. Something more...'

'Romance?'

'Maybe.'

Holly glanced out again at the snow. 'Do you think either of us will have a fairytale romance this Christmas?'

Skye sighed. 'I wish.'

'It's Christmas,' Holly said hopefully. 'A time when wishes can come true.'

They continued to chat and sew, discussing their plans for the following day.

'Are there any festive events on the to–do list?' said Skye.

Holly checked the list pinned up in the kitchen while clearing their cups away. 'The next event we said we'd go to is the lantern walk.'

'I asked Innis if there's any skinny or skimpy dipping at the waterfall. He said no, and seemed

176

surprised that I was up for putting on my swimsuit and braving the cold water.'

'The thought of it makes me shiver.' Holly shuddered. 'What do we have to do?'

'Innis says everyone carries a lantern and walks from the forest road through the snow to the forget–me–not waterfall. A fire pit, like the one at the carol singing, is set up, and there is more hot chocolate and marshmallow toasting.'

'Now that's something I'd like.'

'We'll need our sturdy boots and warm coats, Innis told me.'

'We've got those. What else do we need?'

'The lanterns. That's it.'

Holly checked the note she'd written on the list. 'The night before the lantern walk, we're going to the traditional festive tea at Lyle's shop.'

'His quiche tonight was tasty. I'd happily have more of that and his chocolate Yule log.'

'I told Lyle I've been reading through the recipes in the book he gave me. I just haven't had time to do any baking. But he says I can pop in any evening to the tea shop and learn from him.'

'You should, especially as there's the feeling of Christmas romance in the air.'

Holly laughed, but the warmth she felt in her heart for Lyle gave her hope.

Working late into the evening, they finally tidied up and drove home.

That night, Skye lay tucked up in bed gazing out at the snow. Rewinding the events of the day she drifted off to sleep thinking about Innis...

Driving through the snow on his way back to the castle, Innis had taken a detour through the forest to have a look at thistle loch. The hills around the whole area were blanketed in white. The slopes that were used for the sledging would be perfect for the event.

Heading away, he drove back through the forest to the castle. Lights shone from the windows casting a glow on to the snow that covered the gardens. A ceilidh night that had been held for guests was coming to a close as he walked into the reception, dropped off his winter jacket, and joined Finlay and Ean at their table in the function room. They were wearing their kilts and had been joining in the ceilidh dancing.

Guests filtered out of the party night looking like they'd had a great time and headed to their rooms.

The three brothers sat discussing their plans for the forthcoming ball.

'Brodrick spoke to Nairne and they've sorted out the order for extra ice cream,' said Finlay, running his pen down the to–do list in front of him.

Innis told them about his evening at the tea shop. 'The quiche we had was excellent, so make sure Nairne includes it on the menu.'

Finlay and Ean exchanged a look and smiled.

'What?' said Innis. 'I didn't plan to spend the evening there with Skye. Holly and Skye hadn't eaten dinner and were working late at the dress shop. Brodrick's cafe bar was jumping due to it being one of his Christmas nights, so Lyle invited us all to join him in the tea shop. He was batch baking quiche for his festive tea event.'

Finlay and Ean's smiles broadened.

'And it gave me a chance to try the quiche for myself,' Innis added.

'You and Skye are certainly getting along very well these days,' Finlay remarked, happy for his brother.

'Ailsa says you bought a little something for Skye from her stall at the Christmas market,' Ean added.

'No secrets on this island.' Innis shook his head, but tried not to smile.

'Now we've all got a partner for the ball,' Ean chimed in. 'People have been saying that there's a sense of romance in the air this Christmas. So it's the perfect time to hold a fairytale ball.'

'We should take some pictures of the castle lit up in the snow and put them on the website,' Innis suggested. 'When I drove up it looked picture perfect.'

Ean stood up. 'I'll pop out and take a few before Murdo starts putting the lights out.'

Finlay looked at his list again. 'I think we've more or less got everything in order. Nairne has the menu planned, and the bookings are pouring in, not only for the ball, but for breaks in the New Year and spring weddings. The whole thing has sparked extra interest in the castle, and we were already doing well.'

They stood up and walked out of the function room to head upstairs to their private suites.

Ean came running in from the cold, brushing snowflakes off his white ghillie shirt and dark waistcoat. His legs had braved the icy air but he was used to wearing thick socks and brogues with his kilt and exposing his knees to the wintry weather. Lean and fit from hill running, Ean often raced over the countryside in his kilt as well as his training gear.

'I've got some great shots.' Ean's enthusiasm sounded clear. He showed his brothers the photos on his camera. 'The castle looks magnificent tonight in the first fresh snow of the winter.'

'Excellent,' said Finlay. 'Send them to me and I'll upload them to the website. I've a few things to update, including the new bookings. Nairne has given me a buffet menu list so I'm adding that too.'

Even in the feature Merrilees had written for the newspaper, she'd brushed over the details of the menu and given a general idea of the delicious choices that would be available at the ball.

The three of them walked upstairs talking about their plans. And about Innis and Skye.

Innis tried to make light of it, but his brothers knew him too well.

'It's true what they say,' remarked Ean. 'Opposites do attract. Look at me and Ailsa. I know we have a shared interest in art, but apart from that...' he shrugged.

Innis and Finlay agreed.

'You and Merrilees are a strong match,' Innis told Finlay.

'She's the perfect woman for me,' Finlay told them. 'I see my future with her.'

What did he see for himself with Skye Innis suddenly wondered. He'd started to think past the present, and it had crossed his mind about where they'd live if they ever got married. A thought that had wandered into his dreams recently. Nothing was clear though, maybe because he kept warning himself not to break her heart. But now that he stood on the brink of falling deeply in love with her, if he hadn't already, marriage was on his mind. Everyone expected Finlay or Ean to be the first to marry especially as they were already happily dating Merrilees and Ailsa. As fairly new couples, they seemed to have a lead on him. But maybe...the lone wolf would win that accolade.

Innis shook himself from such deep thoughts and heard the chatter of his brothers return to full volume and clarity...

'So I've promised Merrilees I'll practise with her on the easy slopes. She's done sledging before years ago, but she wants to brush up on it,' said Finlay. 'She's not planning on racing anyone, it's just for fun.'

'It's the same with Ailsa and me,' Ean added.

Innis stopped outside his door and looked at them. 'Skye plans to leave me in a trail of snowflakes as she whizzes past me. She mentioned that tonight at the tea shop.'

Finlay and Ean laughed and then headed to their own rooms.

The winter grey, white and beige decor of Innis' private suite matched the view from the windows. He wandered through to the bedroom and stripped off his clothes. The suite was warm and he stood gazing out at the view wearing grey silk boxers ready for bed.

The front gardens were covered in snow and flakes swirled outside the window as the snowstorm gathered pace. But the snow storm was no match for the castle's thick walls that had withstood many decades of winters.

The view of the sea in the distance was a blur of snowflakes and only the red and yellow lights from the main street's decorations shone through the whiteout.

Winter was well and truly here, and a rush of excitement charged through him. He loved the winters at the castle and the feeling of the festive season on the island.And for a second he let himself picture Skye there with him, cosy and warm together in the castle.

For the first time the warning — *don't break her heart* was beaten by a new consideration — *would Skye break his heart?*

Blinking away this thought, he climbed into bed watching the snow fall until he fell asleep.

The snow clouds across the pale grey sky refused to allow any direct sunlight to shine through. Arching over the town and stretched along the coast and out to sea, the grey sky promised more snow later that morning.

The new delivery of ball gowns had arrived and Skye and Holly's squeal of glee filled their shop along with the beautiful dresses.

The amber confection was claimed by Holly as soon as she saw it and held it up in front of herself to view in the mirror. 'It's even lovelier than I'd hoped.'

'The colour suits your chestnut hair and green eyes.'

Holly nodded and slipped behind the dressing room curtain to try the dress on.

'Zip me up,' Holly stood so Skye could fasten the zipper at the back of the dress.

'There you go.' Skye stepped back to admire the dress. 'It's so lovely. The layers of fabric will make it wonderful for sweeping around the dance floor.'

Holly held the sides of the full skirt and swished them back and forth. 'It glitters with the gold thread.'

Skye studied the satin bodice that was embellished with gold sequins and shiny amber crystals. 'It's as if it was made for you.' She peered at it closely. 'I don't think it's ever been worn.'

'That's what I was thinking,' Holly agreed.

They had enough experience of handling vintage dresses to recognise when a dress had barely been worn. Many of the dresses that found their way into their shop were *worn–once* designs as they called them. After one outing to a party, they'd hung in a wardrobe or been packed away in storage never to see the light again until they'd been acquired for sale in the shop.

Holly viewed the dress from all angles and looked down at the bodice. 'There isn't a sequin or crystal missing that I can see.'

Their shop wasn't open for another half an hour, but Primrose chapped on the window and waved, wanting to come in.

Skye unlocked the door.

'I know you're not open yet,' Primrose began, 'but I want that ball gown you've got on display in the window. I don't care if it's an exact fit or not, I'll make it work.'

They didn't doubt it. Both Primrose and Rosabel were experts in knitting and dressmaking, as well as baking.

'I'll take this dress off and give you a hand to get it off the mannequin,' said Holly.

'Oh, is that the dress you're wearing to the ball?' Primrose's remark made Holly pause and smile. 'Yes, it arrived this morning, but we think it's a never been worn vintage designer dress.'

Primrose went over for a closer look. 'It's perfect on you. The amber colour suits you so well.'

'Thank you, Primrose.' Holly then went to change out of her dress.

'Don't rush. I'll help Skye get the yellow ball gown off the mannequin. It's definitely my colour. And that wispy chiffon and not too plunging a neckline... I want it,' Primrose insisted.

Between them Skye and Primrose wrestled the dress off the mannequin.

'This mannequin takes moods, I'm sure of it,' Skye commented.

Primrose laughed. 'A bit like us. I hear that you and Innis are really getting along.' She called through to Holly in the changing room. 'And you and Lyle.'

'Lyle's teaching me how to bake,' Holly shouted through the curtain that shielded her modesty.

Primrose shot a knowing look at Skye.

Skye giggled.

'What are you two giggling about?' Holly called to them. In the confines of the small changing room it was a battle of wills trying to take the ball gown off without wrestling against herself.

'Learning to bake is a very handy skill,' Primrose commented as Skye lifted the dress over to the counter, folded it carefully and put it into a bag.

Primrose paid for it, and clasped the bag in sheer excitement. 'I saw it last night, thought it over and decided to snap it up before anyone else bought it. Thanks for opening up the shop for me.'

'Do you want to try your dress on?' Holly offered, stepping out of the changing room.

'No, it's fine. As I say, I'll make it work. I'll try it on at home. I can't wait to finish the day at the cake shop and start on it. Rosabel plans to pop in to see the new arrivals.'

'Tell her to come in now. We've just opened the new delivery.'

'I'll do that right now.' Primrose hurried out and headed for the cake shop.

'I'm putting this dress on my currently loved rail,' Holly said, taking it through to the back of the shop.

Rosabel came rushing in. 'Primrose says the new dresses have arrived.'

'Yes, we're still unpacking them. Want to help?' Skye gestured to the two large boxes on the floor of the shop.

Rosabel couldn't wait to help Skye lift each dress out and carefully unfold it and give it a little shake before putting it on a hanger on one of the rails.

Holly picked up the mannequin that was lying prone in the window display. 'Every time we put a dress on her someone buys it.' She wasn't complaining, but it was a bit of a fuss having to keep dressing and undressing the mannequin. They had three mannequins, but the other two were put out of the way because when a full ball gown was on display in the window there wasn't room for any others.

185

Skye had an idea. 'Don't put that green velvet and brocade gown on her.' Skye ran through to her currently loved rail and lifted the pink ball gown through to be put on the mannequin.

'Great idea!' Holly dressed the mannequin while Skye wrote a *display only* note and pinned it up in the window.

'Sorted,' Skye announced standing with her hands firmly on her hips. This morning she wore purple cords tucked into her boots and a lilac jumper. Her hair was pinned up in pleats.

Holly's crushed velvet emerald trousers were a retro seventies design and she wore them with a Fair Isle jumper. Her shiny chestnut hair hung around her shoulders.

'Well, look at this,' Rosabel said, lifting up a rose pink ball gown and gauging it for size. 'I think this one has my name on it.'

Skye and Holly thought it suited her and it was her signature colour so...

'I love the soft chiffon skirt. It's not too full. I wanted something less sticky out, if you know what I mean,' said Rosabel.

'If you need any pink chiffon to make alterations to the dress, we have two rolls of it here,' Skye told Rosabel. 'And yellow if Primrose needs it.'

'That's handy to know.' Rosabel was happy with her purchase and left with the dress in a bag. As they didn't have a chance to price it, they charged the same fair but bargain amount as Primrose's dress.

With two sales done before they'd even opened their shop, Holly put the kettle on. 'We'd better get a cuppa before we open up. We're going to be busy again today.'

The grey sky created a cosy feeling inside the shop, and the fairy lights in the window glowed clearly. When it was bright sunshine, like the previous day, they were outshone by the sunlight.

Sipping their tea, they got on with their day, sorting through the new dresses and continued to mend all the ones they had on sale.

Throughout the morning they were busy with local customers buying the vintage ball gowns.

By lunchtime, Skye phoned Merrilees at stargazer cottage. Merrilees had almost finished writing her novel.

'I've repaired those wee bits on your ball gown,' Skye said to her. 'You can pick it up whenever you want.'

'I'm sort of snowed–in at the cottage,' Merrilees told her. 'Is there any chance you could give the dress to Innis to bring up to the castle tonight after he's finished at the cake shop?'

'Yes, I'll do that,' Skye promised.

'Merrilees is going to look gorgeous in that ice blue crystal dress,' Holly remarked as Skye folded it into a bag.

Skye agreed and then glanced out the window. 'Is that the snow on?'

'Looks like it.'

Skye sighed. 'I wanted a wee wander round the stalls. I saw one selling fairy lights.' The Christmas market was still on and Skye had been too busy to shop at the stalls the previous day.

187

'Go now before the snow gets too heavy and people pack up,' Holly encouraged her.

Skye threw her warm coat and woolly hat on. 'I won't be that long.' She took the bag containing Merrilees' dress with her intending to hand it in to the cake shop on her way back.

The Christmas market stalls were busy and the snow fluttering down gently added to the festive atmosphere.

Skye made a beeline for the fairy lights. They had just what she needed. Two sets of colourful fairy lights that were powered by batteries. 'I'll take these.' She handed them to the seller.

'These will look nice in your dress shop window,' the woman selling them remarked. 'They're handy for displays because they don't need plugged in.'

Skye smiled, paid for them and put them in her shoulder bag. 'Thanks, merry Christmas.'

'You too, Skye.'

As she turned to hurry away she bumped into a tall figure standing in her way. She had been so busy putting the lights in her bag she hadn't noticed him.

'More fairy lights?' There was a smirk in Innis' tone.

'You can never have too much Christmas razzle–dazzle.' Skye's chirpy tone made him smile.

'That looks like you've got a bag full of sparkle.' He peered at the dress bag.

'Ah, this is for Merrilees. She wanted me to give this to you to take up to the castle tonight. She's snowed–in at the cottage.' She handed the bag to him.

'I'd be happy to do that.' Taking charge of the bag, he paused, feeling his senses react to seeing her beautiful face smiling at him.

'Well, I'd better get back to the dress shop to help Holly. Another new load of ball gowns arrived.'

'I noticed the pink dress in the window.'

'Yes, that's mine. I'm wearing it to the ball, so be prepared to be dazzled all evening.'

He looked at her as if she was capable of dazzling him every time he set eyes on her.

A blush rose in her cheeks. 'Okay, I'm heading back to a day of fun and frou–frou.'

'Do I even want to know what that is?' His sensual lips broke into a wry grin.

'Nope.' Skye strode away, glancing back once and casting him a cheeky smile.

His heart melted, and then he went back to the cake shop carrying the dress for Merrilees, wishing he could've spent the day with Skye.

Skye burst into the dress shop, shaking the snow from herself and taking off her coat and hat.

'Did you get what you wanted?' said Holly. She was sitting at the sewing machine hemming one of the dresses.

'Yes, I bought two sets of fairy lights.' She tapped her bag and shrugged it off her shoulder.

'More lights?'

'That's what Innis said.' Skye explained what had happened.

'But he has no idea what I'm up to,' Skye insisted.

'What are you up to?'

Skye dug the lights from her bag. 'These a two little sets of lights, battery powered.'

'Okay, so...'

'Sledge challenge,' Skye reminded her.

'You're up to mischief.'

'Isn't that the plan — skulduggery, mischief and bamboozlement.'

Holly grinned. 'What are you going to do with those lights?'

Skye took a deep breath and sounded excited. 'Well...'

CHAPTER THIRTEEN

Skye rummaged through her sewing basket and pulled out her large pom pom maker.

'The big pom pom maker. Should I be worried?' Holly teased her.

'All the better to hide the little battery pack,' Skye explained. 'I'm going to knit the pink woolly hat with the new yarn and add a set of fairy lights.'

'To distract Innis during the sledging challenge?' Holly clarified.

'That's the plan.'

'Do you think it will work?'

'I have no idea, but I'll certainly look Christmassy.'

They giggled.

'What will you do with the other set of lights?' said Holly.

'Wear them too or drape them on the sledge.'

Ailsa interrupted their scheming. 'It's arrived,' she said to Skye, popping in for a moment. 'I've got it hidden in my shop. Pick it up around closing time.'

'Thanks, Ailsa. I'll do that,' Skye confirmed.

Ailsa glanced at the new dresses and held up her hand. 'No, don't tempt me with any more lovely ball gowns. I spent last night sewing a load of sequins on to mine. It now sparkles like a night sky. I don't need two dresses for the ball.' With that comment, she hurried away.

Ailsa had opted for a deep royal blue ball gown that had a velvet bodice and cascading layers of tulle

191

bedazzled with blue sequins. Everyone agreed that it was perfect for her when she tried it on in the shop the previous day. With her dark hair, pale complexion, blue eyes and lovely figure it was definitely the dress for her.

'What has Ailsa got hidden for you?' Holly gave Skye a suspicious look.

'A wee sledge. Nothing fancy. One that I can use for practise.'

'Where are you going to practise?' The mild concern sounded in Holly's voice. 'Innis will see you if you go anywhere near the castle's estate, and that includes thistle loch.'

'I'm not traipsing all the way to the loch. I don't need to. I'm heading up the hill tonight unless there's a blizzard.'

Holly gulped. 'You're going at night?'

'No one will be up there in the evening. I'll be able to whiz about and get the feel of sledging in the snow.'

Holly frowned. 'But the hill is steep. The slopes at thistle loch are tame in comparison.'

'Exactly. If I can whiz down the hill, the slopes will be a skoosh.'

'I'll go with you to make sure you don't come a cropper.'

'No, you're baking tonight. Don't change your plans. I won't be up there long. I just want a wee go at it to see if I can handle sledging. Besides, our house is on the hillside. It'll be like popping out into the back garden, only a bit higher up. And it's nothing but soft snow over grass and heather.'

Two customers came in, curtailing their conversation.

'That's a smashing ball gown in the window,' one of the women remarked. 'I see it's not for sale, but do you have any others like it?'

'We do.' Holly showed them the rails of gowns and watched their faces light up.

While Holly served them, Skye pushed on with the sewing, mending and alterations while mentally planning her exciting evening excursion.

Innis finished icing the Christmas cakes. He'd baked the traditional fruit cakes, infused with whisky, covered them with a layer of marzipan and then smoothed white icing on top. Fondant holly and berries added a festive touch along with red ribbons tied around the edges.

He tidied up, turned the main lights off, leaving the window display aglow, locked the cake shop for the night and, taking the dress for Merrilees with him, he drove home to the castle. He'd thought about taking a walk up the snowy hill to clear his thoughts, but there was too much work to do. The chocolate orders were piling up and he planned to tackle those in the castle kitchen.

The snow had called it a day as he drove up from the coast to the forest road. Everything, including the castle peering over the tall pines, looked like it was encrusted with snow crystals in the bright moonlight.

He opened the car window to breathe in the cold, fresh air, after a hectic day of baking in the cake shop.

The scent of a crisp, snowy night was something he wished he could capture and bottle.

And he thought about Skye, wondering if she was sewing or knitting at home. He'd seen that the dress shop's main lights were off and they'd closed the shop. They didn't appear to be working late there, so he pictured Skye and Holly would be cosy at home. Maybe Skye would be adding those extra fairy lights to their Christmas decor. He smiled to himself, and a familiar warmth filled his heart just thinking about her.

'Wheee!' Skye squealed as loud as she wanted because there was no one on the hill to hear her. She had it all to herself. She pictured that everyone sensible was at home by the fireside, not whizzing down a snow slope on a cold, wintry night.

But they didn't know what they were missing. This was fun! And quite a workout. Wearing leggings, boots, a thick jumper and padded sports jacket with a woolly hat and gloves, she was well kitted out. She hadn't started knitting the pink hat, so she wore a red one she'd made from the same yarn she was using to knit her jumper.

The pattern for the hat was an easy one she'd made a few times, and she was a fast knitter and knew that the pink yarn would knit up well. She planned to work on it in any spare moments. But right now, it was time to trudge back up the hill with her little sledge for another whiz down the snowy slope.

Holly huffed when she looked at her crumbly fruit scones. She'd done something wrong. Checking the recipe, she couldn't figure out what it was. And why was her dried fruit not as plump and delicious as Lyle's?

He'd told her to phone him if she needed baking tips. But it was getting late. While she swithered what to do, another message came through from Skye letting her know she was okay.

Holly was happy for Skye, but less than pleased with her scones. She went to put her phone away and then wondered...

Lyle was locking the front door of his tea shop when his phone rang. He smiled when he saw that it was Holly calling him.

'Holly, what can I do for you?'

She rattled off what was wrong with her scones.

'I'm on my way,' Lyle said, figuring he'd drop by and show Holly how to improve her scones and plump up her sultanas.

It was her own fault. Skye sighed wearily as she lay prone on the snow. Trying to spin the sledge while sliding down the slope didn't work out as planned.

Spluttering and muttering, she picked herself up and brushed as much of the snow off as she could, but she was covered in it. She felt like one of the snowman cookies Holly had baked and dipped in white icing and crystallised sugar.

Innis handed the bag containing the ball gown to Finlay at the castle's reception.

'Skye gave me Merrilees' dress.'

Finlay was pleased. 'I'll call her. She'll be pleased it's here. She plans to get dressed for the ball at the castle rather than at the cottage. I'm keeping it for her in my wardrobe.'

Murdo walked by loaded with lanterns. 'I'll put these in the storeroom ready for the lantern walk.'

'Thanks, and can you make sure we've got extra candles to put in them,' said Finlay.

'Will do,' Murdo assured him and hurried away.

'Are you going on the lantern walk?' Finlay said to Innis.

'I hadn't planned to.'

Ean joined them, overhearing their conversation. 'Ailsa and I are going, and she says that Holly and Skye have bought their lanterns.'

Innis changed his mind. 'Okay, I'll go if we're all going.' Ignoring the smiles exchanged between Finlay and Ean, he headed through to the kitchen to work on his chocolates.

'I steep my dried fruit in an infusion of cold, strong tea,' Lyle told Holly as they stood in her kitchen. 'It plumps up the fruit and adds to the flavour.'

'I'll try that,' Holly said as he went over the scone recipe with her.

'Did you sift your flour?'

'Yes,' she said firmly.

'Was your butter cold?'

'Hmmm, I'd sat it out when I was buttering toast for Skye. I've mastered making my own butter, and I wanted her to have something to eat to keep up her energy when she—' She cut short what she was saying and buttoned her lips.

'Is Skye up to mischief?'

'It's a secret.'

'I won't tell anyone. You can trust me.'

Holly felt the warmth of their growing friendship. She did trust Lyle.

'Promise you won't tell Innis.'

He held up his hand. 'I promise.'

As Holly began to explain about Skye's derring–do up the hill with her sledge, a walking icicle came crunching through the back door into the kitchen.

Skye saw Lyle standing there with Holly, but she was so freeeezing cold she didn't care to question why he was there.

'Oh, dear.' Holly rushed over to her.

'I'm fine. Everything went well until the last slide down the slope. I tried a tricky technique and...' She shrugged, letting her appearance explain.

'Come on, let's get you out of those clothes.' Holly ushered Skye through to the hall, leaving Lyle in the kitchen.

While Holly helped Skye off with her jacket, hat, mitts and boots in the hall, fetched her cosy slippers and a blanket, Lyle knew his way around any kitchen and rustled up three mugs of tea.

'Get a heat by the fire.' Holly sat Skye down by the fireside and wrapped the blanket around her shoulders. 'Your hair will defrost in a few minutes.'

'Thanks, Holly. I don't mean to be a bother. Or interrupt your night with Lyle,' she whispered.

'I had a baking emergency,' Holly summarised.

197

Lyle walked in with a tray of tea and sat it down on the table by the fire. 'Holly's butter wasn't cold enough and I think she'd overmixed her ingredients.' He handed a mug of tea to Skye. 'Take a wee sip. I've added extra milk so you can drink it now.'

'You're so thoughtful, Lyle.' Skye smiled up at him, and then glanced at Holly standing close beside him. And in that instant, she saw the happy couple they were going to be and smiled again. She sipped her tea and relaxed. 'I can feel my cheeks start to thaw.'

'What about your face?' Holly teased her.

Skye laughed.

Then the three of them sat by the fire, drinking their tea and chatting.

Innis worked on creating his chocolates in the castle kitchen. At first, Nairne and other staff had been there, but now he was on his own after they'd finished catering for the guests that evening.

Ean came in with an offer for Innis. 'Finlay is helping Merrilees practise sledging near her cottage at thistle loch tomorrow night. Ailsa and I are joining them. Would you like to come along? Maybe invite Skye?'

Innis liked the feeling that they were starting to be considered as a couple. 'Okay, I'll phone her. Thanks, Ean.'

'Is that some of your new festive chocolates?' Ean lingered, eyeing up the truffles.

'Help yourself,' he gestured to a selection on a tray. He'd boxed the others and the luxury quality of them was evident. 'I'm on a roll tonight. I've caught up with the orders.'

'I don't want to leave you short.'

'These are extra. Take a couple, and Finlay likes the ones with the milk chocolate.'

Ean popped four chocolates on a napkin and bit into one as he left. 'Cheers, Innis' he mumbled.

Taking out his phone, Innis called Skye. Be direct, he told himself. She was a night owl, like him, and a lark, so he thought she'd still be up.

Skye's phone rang. She'd tucked it beside her on her chair by the fire while she knitted. Thawed out, she'd made a start on her pink woolly hat, casting on the stitches and working the first few rows.

'It's Innis,' she told Holly and Lyle.

They looked surprised. Had he found out about her escapade earlier?

'Hello, Innis.'

'Merrilees and Ailsa are planning to practise sledging near thistle loch. Finlay and Ean will be there too. We've been invited. Do you want to go?'

Skye's heart answered an immediate yes. 'When?'

'Tomorrow night, if you're free.'

Her heart sank. 'I'm going to the tea shop tomorrow evening. Holly and I have booked a table for Lyle's special traditional festive event.'

She felt his disappointment reverberate across the distance between them.

'It's fine,' he said.

'I would've loved to have gone sledging with you,' she insisted.

'Another time, Skye. Enjoy your evening at the tea shop.' He tried to sound polite.

She shared his disappointment, but she didn't want to cancel her previous engagement.

Thinking his call was too abrupt, he attempted to chat for a moment. 'What are you up to?'

'Knitting by the fire.' This wasn't a lie, but it gave the wrong impression that she'd been behaving herself all evening and having a cosy night in. If he knew what she'd really be up to...

'I'll let you get on with your knitting. Goodnight, Skye.'

Sighing, she clicked her phone off.

'Bad timing,' Holly commiserated.

'Or maybe great timing.' Lyle tilted the balance in Skye's favour.

Skye and Holly frowned at him.

'If it's skulduggery you're planning, perhaps you're better not playing your hand. Enter the sledging challenge as a wildcard. Innis won't know what to expect.'

Skye brightened at Lyle's reasoning. 'You're right. A wildcard move is more my style.' Feeling better at turning down a sledging date with Innis, she continued knitting her hat.

'I'd better be on my way.' Lyle stood up and stretched. 'Mischief and bamboozlement aside, I had a nice time.'

'Thanks for coming to rescue me and my wonky scones.' Holly walked him to the front door. 'And for helping me bake better in our ordinary wee kitchen.'

Lyle turned up the collar of his warm jacket and stepped outside. 'Remember, in an ordinary kitchen you can bake extraordinary things.'

The freezing cold air blew in, rising up from the sea to where the house was perched halfway up the hill. Ailsa's cottage was nearby, and Brodrick's property.

'Close the door,' Lyle insisted as he hurried to his car. 'Don't let all the heat out.'

Holly closed it and ran through to wave to him out the lounge window.

'You really like him, don't you?' Skye said, knitting another row of her pink hat.

Holly watched the tail lights of Lyle's car disappear into the night. 'A wee bitty.'

Skye's knitting needles worked at speed, clicking in the quietude. She gave Holly a knowing look.

'Okay, maybe a smidgen more than that,' Holly admitted.

'I've given Geneen and Murdo the night off so they can attend the ball,' Finlay said to Innis, wandering into the kitchen eating one of the milk chocolate truffles.

Innis was tidying away his chocolatier work and planning to head up to his suite.

'I'm glad. They seemed like they were going to be a couple when they were paired up at the fashion show.'

'When I told Murdo a few minutes ago, he dashed to talk to Geneen before she finished up at reception for the night. I overheard him invite her to go with him. And then he bounded away to the storeroom. Geneen assumed she'd be on duty for the ball. Now she's planning to buy a dress from Skye and Holly's shop.'

They smiled.

Innis told him about Skye not being available to go to the practise sledging.

'We could arrange it for the night after that,' Finlay suggested, willing to reschedule it.

Innis shook his head. 'Lantern walk.'

Finlay sighed. 'The time is going in so fast until we have the ball on Christmas Eve.' And then he added. 'At least you'll see Skye at the lantern walk. And at the challenge on the slopes.'

'Yes, and at the ball.'

'Are you wearing your dress kilt? The ones we wear for weddings and special events?' Finlay said to him. He planned to wear his.

'I am.' The entire outfit was hanging in his wardrobe.

'So is Ean.' Finlay started to walk away as Innis turned the main lights off, leaving a few spotlights on for the night porter to use the kitchen for himself and for the needs of guests.

'Are you buying Skye something special for Christmas?' Finlay said as they walked upstairs.

'A Christmas present?'

'Yes. I've done my Christmas shopping and I've bought a few things for Merrilees. Ean has done the same for Ailsa. I just wondered...'

'I haven't bought Skye's present yet. But I plan to soon.'

Finlay looked impressed. 'You sound like you have something special in mind.'

'I do.'

Finlay knew when not to pry. 'I hope this Christmas works out for you and Skye.'

'So do I. I'm not buying her a ring if that's what you're thinking. I don't want to get ahead of myself and take things too far too fast.'

Finlay appreciated knowing this, but there was still an underlying plan that he sensed Innis was up to. Whatever it was, Christmas was a time when wishes came true. He wished for happiness for all of them.

CHAPTER FOURTEEN

Snow glittered in the morning sunlight and Skye and Holly's dress shop was busy with customers buying ball gowns. Some of them were buying fabric to alter or upgrade the dresses themselves.

The day flew in and as an early twilight settled over the main street, Skye and Holly got ready to go to the tea shop for dinner.

Innis had been equally busy, baking cakes and decorating them with icing or chocolate ganache. He hadn't seen Skye all day as she'd spent most of it working at her sewing machine. But he had seen her beautiful pink ball gown in the window of the dress shop. He couldn't wait for the night of the ball so he could hold her in his arms and dance with her.

The gift he'd ordered for her from the mainland was due to arrive the following day. He hoped she would like it.

Rosabel and Primrose had been helping with the extra cake baking while leaving the expert icing to Innis.

He heard them chatting about sewing their dresses for the ball, and apparently Geneen had bought her gown from the vintage dress shop.

Working away in the kitchen he listened to the customers talking about getting their groceries and gifts all set for Christmas, and the time seemed to ramp up until it was officially closing time at the cake shop.

Rosabel and Primrose headed home to finish their dresses, waving and telling Innis not to work too late.

But this was his plan, to continue working at the shop, baking, icing and creating everything from traditional Christmas cakes to rich chocolate sponges filled with buttercream, iced with fondant and topped with a couple of his chocolate truffles.

Tucked away in his kitchen, he didn't see how lively the tea shop looked all lit up and with every table taken. He'd considered going along, but checking Lyle's website he saw that the night was fully booked.

He pictured Skye and Holly sitting at their window table looking out at the sea view while being feted by Lyle and his tasty tea shop menu.

Innis had checked the menu, something he often did, not for competitive purposes, but out of interest in what was popular with customers. Lyle had highlighted his special Yule log, his own recipe that he said was rich with chocolate flavour.

Skye gazed out the tea shop window at the wintry sea as she enjoyed her Yule log with Holly. There was a wildness to the sea that appealed to her. It looked especially beautiful against the snowy night.

'This Yule log is delicious,' Holly said to Skye.

Lyle overheard her as he buzzed around serving customers. He'd hired a couple of staff to help him, and the atmosphere in the upstairs extension was warm and welcoming.

'Thank you, Holly,' said Lyle. 'It's my special recipe.'

Holly pointed her fork at the cake. 'I don't know what you've added to the chocolate ganache topping to make it taste so rich.'

'Extra dark chocolate, extra cream and a pinch of spice,' Lyle confided.

Skye nodded as she ate hers.

'I'm baking some for the ball's buffet,' he added.

'Great,' said Holly.

Bustling around, Lyle kept swinging by their table, adding little extras including chocolate dipped cherries and sugared Scottish raspberries to their cake stand.

They'd started with the quiche and salad, moved on to the scones with whipped cream and strawberry jam, and finished with the Yule log and dipped fruits.

Hastily made tomato sandwiches was all they'd had for lunch due to being so busy at their shop. This ensured they had an appetite for the traditional tea shop treats.

Skye couldn't help her thoughts drifting to the sledging practise that Merrilees and Ailsa would be enjoying near thistle loch with Finlay and Ean. And as much as she was flattered that Innis had invited her to go with him, she was happy to be at the tea shop with Holly.

Innis finally finished work at the cake shop. Glancing out the window, he saw the wild sea. But it wasn't snowing, so he put his warm jacket and boots on and instead of driving home to the castle, he ventured up the hill to clear his thoughts.

The view from the top was always worth it. The main street far below glittered with fairy lights and the large Christmas tree glowed like a beacon.

The icy breeze blew through his hair, sweeping it back from his troubled brow. Troubled because he wondered about getting deeply involved with Skye. He was involved already even though they weren't officially a couple.

He'd see her at the lantern walk. Finlay, Merrilees, Ean and Ailsa were planning to set off from the castle, cutting through a part of the forest that led to the waterfall. Others would be walking up the forest road from the coast route and approaching the waterfall from that direction.

Innis planned to leave the castle along with Finlay and the others. No doubt Skye and Holly would be accompanied by Lyle, but once they all met up at the waterfall, he hoped to spend the time there with Skye.

And then it wouldn't be long until the snow challenge. He was disappointed that Skye hadn't been able to join in the practise with Merrilees and the others. Skye had never done any sledging and this put her at a further disadvantage.

The wind rising up from the sea whipped up the fallen snow sending flakes circling around him like starlight. There was a sense of fairytale magic in the air, or perhaps he was just falling deeper under Skye's spell.

Before trudging back down the hill, he looked way off in the distance towards the estate. The dark silhouette of the castle stood strong against the elements. He felt this was what he needed to do if he wanted to win Skye's heart — stand strong against the twists and turns of events that at times seemed to conspire to keep them apart.

With that bolstering thought, Innis tugged up the collar of his jacket and bounded back down the hill with more determination than when he went up it.

Another day sparkled under the winter light and flew by again in a blaze of ball gowns and glittering sequins.

Skye arranged the ball gowns that were left on the rails along with the evening dresses, while Holly parcelled up online orders that were mainly for the evening dresses and little cocktail numbers.

'What should we wear for the lantern walk?' said Holly as she packed the dresses.

'Warm coats, warm trousers, warm boots, warm...everything,' Skye advised her.

Holly peered out the window at the grey clouds swirling along the coast. 'Do you think it could rain and our lanterns will fizzle out in the wet?'

'Nope. The forecast is more snow.'

'It was wrong before,' Holly reminded her.

'The forecast according to Innis,' Skye clarified. She'd met him briefly when she'd popped out for milk for tea. He was outside his shop loading cake and chocolate boxes into the back of his car. They'd chatted for a moment, mainly about the weather and the lantern walk.

'Warm everything it is then,' said Holly. No argument from her.

The snow held off, as if doing them the courtesy of not forcing those taking part in the lantern walk to trudge through a blizzard.

In rows of two or three, everyone walked along the forest road carrying their lanterns.

Many of them had left their cars down at the main street to walk the entire route, while others living inland, like Rory, had parked at the forest road.

Lyle accompanied Holly and Skye, and they chatted about everything from baking mince pies to waltzing at the castle.

Ahead of them were Rory and Rowen. He'd bought the lovely ball gown Rowen had selected from the dress shop, and he'd told Skye that he was wearing a classic dinner suit to attend the ball.

Geneen had revealed when she'd been in buying her dress that Innis, Finlay and Ean were wearing their full kilts and finery. And that they always went commando under their kilts. Something neither Skye or Holly wanted to ponder.

Behind Skye and the others were Elspeth and Brodrick, followed by Morven and Donall. Somewhere near them walked Nettie and Shuggie, and someone said they heard contented purring from Shuggie's backpack.

Rosabel and Primrose were near the front and had taken part in a few lantern walks over the years.

There was a fine turnout for the event from the local community and the cold air was abuzz with their joy at being out at night in the snow with their lanterns looking like festive firelight in the depths of winter.

As they all veered off the main forest road into the heart of the forest itself, Skye glanced back at the view of the sea in the distance. She'd only seen it from the car, but walking along gave a different perspective and she saw even more rugged beauty in the island's wild landscape.

The air changed to a stillness as the thick trees shielded them from the worst of the cold wind.

Skye held up her lantern. The candlelight was steady rather than flickering in the breeze. The dark forest route opened out on to forget–me–not waterfall all aglow with lights.

The fire pit was set up by the organisers and was burning brightly, ready for them to toast marshmallows to go with their hot chocolate.

Lights illuminated the cascading waterfall and the pool it collected in shone with lights too. Some were coloured turquoise blue or pink, creating a fantasy feeling.

Fairy lights had been entwined through the surrounding greenery, and people were starting to take photos of the extraordinary beauty.

Lyle stepped back and took out his phone. 'Stand together in front of the waterfall,' he said to Skye and Holly, and proceeded to snap several great photos of them together, something they'd treasure.

Skye then used her phone to take pictures of Holly and Lyle together. At first, Lyle was careful not to pose as if he was Holly's boyfriend, but by the time Skye had finished, Holly and Lyle had their arms wrapped around each other and were grinning at her.

Scrolling through the pictures, Skye then showed them to Holly and Lyle. Perhaps it was seeing themselves as a couple that helped them to take their friendship to the next level.

'I know I'm an acquired taste,' Lyle began, 'but would you like to go to the ball with me, Holly?'

'I'd love to.'

While Holly and Lyle toasted marshmallows together, Skye wandered over to the waterfall and gazed at the lights glistening through the cascading water. Glancing round at the sound of other voices, she saw that Innis and his brothers along with Merrilees and Ailsa had arrived. Their route from the castle made them approach from a different direction through the trees.

Innis' eyes scanned around everyone present and then locked on to Skye.

She smiled at him as he walked over to her. Warmly dressed in a classic winter jacket, cords and sturdy boots, her heart reacted seeing him. Finlay and Ean were equally kitted out in winter wear but they both wore woolly hats. Innis didn't, and his dark hair was flecked with a few snowflakes that had fallen from the trees as they'd walked through the forest.

He carried his lantern and his voice sounded deep in the cold air. 'Did you enjoy your night at the tea shop?'

'I did.' Skye gave him a brief description of the menu and the evening.

She then asked him about his evening, wondering if he'd joined in the sledging.

'No, I worked late at the shop and then went for a walk up the hill. I had it all to myself as usual. It helps me to unwind, get some fresh air if I've been baking in the shop all day, and I've always loved the view of the island from the top.'

Skye kept her bright smile steady, while thinking how close she'd come to encountering Innis on the hill when she'd been sledging.

'Would you like to go for a walk?' Innis' amber eyes reflected the flames from the fire. 'There's something I'd like to show you.'

Skye drank down the remainder of her hot chocolate. 'Lead the way,' she said sprightly.

'Bring your lantern.' He carried his.

Leaving the others to enjoy the waterfall, Innis forged through an archway in the trees.

Skye held her lantern ahead of her, following close to Innis as he swept aside some branches and dipped his head under the archway.

'I get the feeling this is a secret route to somewhere that you've known for years,' she commented, noticing the surefooted way he navigated it.

'I've used it since I was a boy.' He brushed aside a low hanging branch. 'Though the archway seemed a lot higher then.'

He glanced at her over his shoulder and a wry smile played on his lips.

'Where are we going?' She saw nothing but the depths of the forest all around them. It was so dense it cut out the icy breeze and there was a calming stillness to the atmosphere. A dreamlike quality, like a rustic fairytale.

'Nearly there,' he assured her. Pushing the last branches aside, the forest archway opened out on to the countryside around thistle loch.

She gasped. 'We're at thistle loch? Already?'

'The archway is a racing line to the loch. I thought you'd like to see where you'll be sledging. As you haven't had a chance to practise, I thought you should at least have a clear picture of it in your mind. The landscape is quite vast and some people find that overwhelming until they get used to it.'

Skye stood beside him and felt the rush of cold air now blow through her hair that tumbled from underneath her woolly hat. His broad shoulders and tall stature helped shield her from the brunt of the gusts that swept across the loch unchallenged.

He gestured over to the area of long, but low hills from the depths of the countryside that ran down to the loch, levelling out before they reached the water.

'The slopes for the sledging are deceiving. They're not too steep, but you can pick up a fair pace sledging down them.'

'They look a lot less steep than—' she bit her lip, almost letting slip that she was comparing them to the hill.

'Than what?' he prompted her.

'Than I thought they would,' she fibbed.

'No one ever overruns the slope and ends up in the loch in case you're wondering,' he told her.

It hadn't crossed her mind. She was too busy calibrating how fast she'd need to go to beat him.

213

Whizzing down these vast but reasonably gentle slopes seemed doable and stirred her competitive streak.

Then her attention was drawn to the little cottage in the distance on the other side of the loch and partly bordered by trees. Stargazer cottage where Merrilees stayed. The windows were in darkness, but a lantern glowed at the side of the front door, burning a constant welcome home.

Innis followed her line of vision. 'That's Merrilees cottage.'

Skye nodded. She knew.

'It's temporary, until she marries Finlay and moves into the castle,' he explained.

Skye didn't give away what she was thinking, so he took the chance to pry.

'What about you? Are you of a mind to settle down one day? Get married?'

The mercurial side of her nature rose up to reply. 'Sometimes, yes, other times...it seems like it's so far in the distance that I can't quite grasp it. Always out of reach.'

The blood coursed through his veins as he fought the urge to tell her he was right there, standing beside her, and he always would be.

Before he could say anything, she threw the same question back at him.

He heard his reply and thought it was the mirror image of hers. 'I've been thinking since earlier this year that I'd like to settle down. Get married. Folk keep telling me that the woman for me will one day arrive on the island.' He didn't dare look at her and kept his gaze steady on the snow slopes. 'But I'm now thinking that she could've been here for a while.'

Skye glanced up at him, but he didn't falter in his outward focus.

A flurry of snow and a gust of wind blew with force across the loch, jarring them.

Innis frowned as he glanced up at the fast–moving storm clouds blustering up from the coast and from inland, arching over the loch and surrounding landscape.

Skye gazed up and directly above her a storm appeared to be brewing.

'We'd better get back to the waterfall and give the others fair warning.'

Skye's eyes widened, glancing between Innis and the approaching storm. 'Is it rain or snow?'

'A snowstorm. And it's about to hit the island soon.'

Innis strode ahead, eager to get back to the waterfall.

Skye struggled to keep pace with his long, capable strides.

'Come on, Skye,' he beckoned her.

'My furry boots are slowing me down.' It wasn't an excuse. They weren't snow hiking boots, just fashionably furry and kept her warm, but they weren't made for speed. The snow became deeper on the route back to the forest archway.

Innis took charge of the situation and keeping a grip on his lantern he lifted her up in his strong arms, carrying her without faltering in his stride.

Clasping her lantern, she put one arm around his shoulders and held tight, though she had no fear that he'd drop her. His strength and protectiveness ignited her senses. She felt safe with Innis. She was safe with him.

At the archway he put her down gently and then wasted no time leading them through the forest back to the clearing at the waterfall.

Voices singing carols sounded long before they saw the cheery faces, singing, drinking hot chocolate and toasting marshmallows.

Innis loathed calling a halt to their fun night, but he knew they'd understand.

'A snowstorm is on its way,' Innis announced.

They could tell from his no nonsense tone that they needed to pack up and head home. No one complained. Common sense prevailed.

The organisers dowsed the fire pit, grabbed the items they'd brought and got going.

'My taxi is parked down the forest road,' said Shuggie. 'Anyone wanting a lift down to the main street, come with me and Nettie.'

Innis encouraged Rosabel and Primrose to go in the taxi.

There was no time for anyone to argue. Those living locally knew the island enjoyed mainly mild weather, but there were times in the deep midwinter when the snow could be a challenge.

Innis kept Skye close to him as he rounded everyone up. 'Is everyone accounted for?' His commanding voice sounded clear.

Those present nodded, making sure no one had gone amiss.

'My car is near Shuggie's taxi,' Rory told them, keeping a clasp of Rowen's hand. 'Some folk can come with us. I'm dropping Rowen off and then heading inland near the farms.'

A couple were keen to take up Rory's offer, and they headed away with him.

Others divided themselves among the remaining cars and hurried off.

'Don't wait for us,' Finlay told them. 'Get going now.'

'I'll walk Holly and Skye back down to the main street,' Lyle told Innis. 'You get back to the castle with your brothers.'

But before they could decide, Brodrick stepped in. 'The three of you can jump in my car with Elspeth and me.'

A firm nod and Brodrick, clasping Elspeth's hand, started to head away.

Skye went to follow, but Innis stepped close to her for a moment and gazed into her eyes. 'Don't do anything foolish. Phone me when you get home. Let me know you're safe.'

'I will. What about you?'

'I'm going back to the castle. Sometimes guests wander off around the estate and we need to ensure they're all in for the night,' Innis explained quickly.

Skye thought for a moment that Innis was going to kiss her, and she was right, but he stopped himself, not wanting their first kiss of passion to be in the midst of a melee.

217

Accompanying Finlay, Merrilees, Ean and Ailsa back to the castle through the forest, Innis rewound the moments he'd had with Skye at thistle loch. The snowstorm had curtailed their evening. The storm would pass, but he sensed that his feelings for Skye were all the stronger for their time together.

CHAPTER FIFTEEN

Skye and Holly hurried inside their house out of the cold after Brodrick dropped them off. He'd already dropped Lyle outside the tea shop. Waving to them and insisting he was used to the snow, Lyle drove off home.

They hung their coats up in the hall and Holly lit the fire.

While Holly added kindling, Skye phoned Innis.

'We're home safe,' Skye told him as promised.

'Thanks for letting me know. We've ensured all the guests are inside the castle. It's going to be a stormy night, so keep warm,' Innis advised. 'This type of snowstorm usually hits during the night and the worst of it is gone by the morning. Everything will be covered in extra snow, but it'll make the slopes perfect for the sledging.'

'Still up for the challenge?' There was teasing in her tone.

'I am,' he replied firmly. 'Unfortunately, I'm going to be extremely busy with the cake shop and helping Finlay and Ean get everything ready for the ball. You probably won't see much of me until the sledging challenge.'

Skye knew she was going to be crazy busy too. 'See you on the slopes,' she said.

After finishing the call Skye flopped down on the sofa.

Holly warmed her hands by the fire. 'Does Innis know that you turned yourself into a sugar cookie when you were up the hill in the snow?'

'No, but I nearly blurted it out myself this evening when we were talking up at thistle loch.'

Holly laughed. 'You're rubbish at keeping secrets, even your own.'

Skye didn't disagree. 'Innis brought up the subject of settling down — and marriage.'

'He talked to you about getting married?'

'Well...he skirted around the topic, gauging my reaction, wondering if I was interested in settling down and getting married.' Skye told her the details.

'It sounds like Innis is hooked on you. Lyle and I noticed the way he looks at you.'

'I heard Lyle invite you to go with him to the ball.' Skye nudged the conversation away from herself.

Holly blushed.

'You're blushing,' Skye teased her.

'It's the heat from the fire.'

Skye threw her a look of disbelief.

'Okay, so I'm going to the ball with Lyle. But you're changing the subject. Tell me more about what happened with you and Innis at thistle loch.'

'When he noticed the storm coming, we started to hurry back, but my boots were slowing me down in the deep snow so Innis lifted me up and carried me part of the way.'

'Oooh! How chivalrous of him.'

Skye laughed. 'He's very strong. I'm going to have to try extra skulduggery to beat him on the slopes. Are you challenging Lyle?'

'No, we've agreed to just have fun and leave the mischief–making to you.'

'Smart move.' Skye reached for her knitting bag, pulled out the partially finished pink hat and continued to follow the pattern and knit a few rows before they got ready for bed.

'Are those more pom poms you've been making?' Holly peered into the knitting bag.

'I had plenty of spare white yarn so...'

'Why do you need all those pom poms for your woolly hat?'

'They're not for my hat. I've already made the large pink one for the top.' Skye held it up like an exhibit. It was large, pink and she'd made it extra fluffy with a teasel brush.

'What are the white pom poms for then?' said Holly.

'They're fake snowballs. For the challenge,' Skye told her succinctly. 'Let's see Innis dodge these.'

Holly laughed. 'You're going to hurl woolly pom poms at him?'

'Bamboozlement technique.'

'Lyle was right,' Holly conceded.

'About what?'

'That Innis won't stand a chance against you on the slippery slopes.'

Skye smiled.

Holly glanced at the snow falling outside the window. She got up and went over to peer out. Skye put her knitting down and joined her.

Snow was sweeping along the coast like a blizzard.

'I'm glad we got home when we did,' said Holly.

'Yes,' Skye agreed.

'Oh, I meant to tell you, at the waterfall tonight, Finlay invited us to join them at the castle for the traditional festive meal on Christmas Day.'

'You and me?'

'And Lyle. Finlay and Ean will be there with Merrilees and Ailsa. He's invited Rory and Rowen too. We're all invited as friends to join them at their private table in the function room where the guests will be having their Christmas dinner.'

Skye was delighted.

'I said yes. You were away with Innis. But I thought you'd love to spend Christmas Day at the castle.'

'That would be wonderful. It means that after the ball on Christmas Eve, the celebrations aren't over.'

'A fairytale ball and then a fairytale Christmas on the island.'

'What will we wear on Christmas Day?' Skye sounded excited.

Holly frowned jokingly. 'I don't know. There must be a shop that sells dresses.'

They laughed.

'There's that red velvet dress hanging on your currently loved rail in the shop,' Skye reminded her.

'And the emerald velvet and satin fifties wrap dress,' Holly remembered.

'I've never worn the rose tea dress that's on my rail. Or the vintage pink brocade dress.'

'Fortunately, it's snowing or we'd be running down to the shop to try them on.'

Skye peered out the window at the snowstorm and pretended to make light of it. 'We could tackle the blizzard.'

Holly balked at this idea for a moment and then realised that Skye was winding her up.

'Come on, it's getting late, we really should get some sleep.'

Holly agreed. 'Especially if we've more dresses for Christmas at the castle to sort out in the morning.'

'And scheming and mischief to plan,' Skye reminded her.

'We're going to be busy.'

'It'll make the time fly in until it's the sledging challenge.' Skye rubbed her hands together with glee.

'I definitely agree with Lyle,' Holly reiterated, putting the guard up in front of the fire and turning the lounge lights off. 'Innis won't stand a chance against you.'

The time did fly in.

In the hustle and bustle of Christmas shopping, carol singing, dress selecting and posting out the last minute orders to their customers, Skye and Holly were now getting wrapped up warm in their winter wear to tackle the snowy slopes.

Lyle offered to drive them up to thistle loch and they'd taken him up on this.

Holly sat up front with Lyle while Skye sat in the back and wrestled with the fairy lights she'd entwined in her pink woolly hat. The large, fluffy pom pom hid the little battery pack, and the lights poked through the knitting in a colourful display.

'Shield your eyes,' Skye joked. 'I'm about to turn the fairy lights on to test if they're working.'

Lyle lowered the visor in front of him. 'In case of dazzling flashback.'

'They work!' Skye yelled. She switched them off to save the battery power.

'What have you got tucked in your jacket pockets?' Lyle said to Skye.

'You noticed?'

'The last time I saw bulges like that a squirrel was stashing nuts in his cheeks,' said Lyle.

'It's her pom poms,' Holly explained.

'Ah, do I even want to know what you're going to do with them?' he said.

'Nooo,' Skye told him.

Laughter and chatter filled the car on the drive up the forest road and on to thistle loch where the countryside was blanketed in snow.

Lyle parked alongside other cars and stepped out into the fairly deep snow. He was well kitted out in sporty snow gear and boots.

'Careful when you step out,' he said, making sure neither of them took a tumble before they'd even started sledging.

The afternoon sunlight was forcing through the vast grey sky that arched over the entire area, from the loch to the hills rising up into the surrounding countryside.

There were practise slopes for total beginners where Skye would've started if she hadn't challenged Innis. Squeals of delight rang clear in the cold, crisp air and there was a stillness that created an atmosphere that was perfect for sledging.

The main slopes, including the most daring one, were covered in snow. After the blizzard, Innis had been right. It had faded by the morning but left its mark in a whiteout over the island. But this ensured that the snow for the sledging was fresh.

There were no trees, rocks or other natural obstacles on the slopes, giving the participants a clear run down the hills.

'There's Innis over by the slopes.' Lyle gestured in the direction. 'I think he's seen us arrive.'

'He's got our sledges,' Skye said to Holly. The pink sledge and the turquoise blue one stood out against the whiteout.

Lyle took his sledge out of the boot of his car. He'd used it for the past few years.

'Shall we head over?' Lyle pulled his sledge behind him and walked alongside Holly.

Skye lingered a little behind, hoping to hide the fairy lights in her hat and through the woolly scarf she was wearing by keeping her distance.

'Is Skye okay?' Innis said to Holly and Lyle.

'Yes, totally fine,' Holly assured him.

Innis wasn't assured in the slightest. 'What's she got in her jacket pockets?' He peered against a beam of sunlight streaming through the cold air.

Holly didn't have an immediate reply, so Lyle spoke up.

'Padding,' Lyle told him in a voice that sounded reasonable. 'In case she takes a tumble.'

Holly backed Lyle up. 'Yes, Skye doesn't have much experience of sledging, so she's padded up.'

Innis frowned. 'I thought she didn't have any experience.'

'That's what I mean,' Holly blustered. 'Is that our sledges? I assume the pink one is for Skye.'

'It is. The blue one is for you.' Innis handed her the cord of the blue sledge.

Holly fussed with her sledge, trying to distract Innis from studying Skye too closely. 'I'll take Skye's over to her. I think she's adjusting her...eh, padding.'

Hurrying as fast as she could in snow boots, Holly pulled the pink sledge over to Skye, leaving Lyle in charge of the blue one.

Lyle kept Innis talking. 'So, what do you suggest are the fun and fastest runs?'

Innis switched into information mode, happy to extol the benefits of the various slopes. 'The fun slopes are those three over there.'

'Those look busy,' Lyle commented. 'But Holly and I are here for the fun, not to race. Though I believe you and Skye are about to go head to head on the slopes.'

Put like that, it made Innis feel like he shouldn't have encouraged their challenge and should've opted for fun like Lyle and Holly. 'Perhaps I should cancel the challenge.'

'No, don't do that,' Lyle insisted. 'Skye's been looking forward to it. She'll be disappointed if you back out now.'

Innis felt like there was trouble to the right of him and chaos to the left. He'd got himself into a double–pincer trap of his own making.

Holly came trudging back over to Lyle and Innis. 'Skye says we should head up to the hills. She'll join us in a few minutes. She's taking a phone call from one of our suppliers.'

'Right,' Innis sounded thwarted. 'Let's head up to the fast slopes.'

Keeping Innis' thoughts occupied while Skye trudged from a slightly different direction towards the slopes, Holly told Innis that they were all happy to have Christmas dinner at the castle.

'You'll all be welcome,' said Innis, glancing back to see where Skye had gone.

'Is this one of the sledges from the castle that the guests use?' Holly said to distract Innis.

'It is. The guests enjoy getting out into the snow.'

Skye sat on her sledge, adjusted her lights, and armed herself with two pom poms in her feisty fist ready to throw them at Innis as they set off. Her plan was to knock him off his sledging stride from the get–go.

'It looks like Skye is ready to take you on right now, Innis,' Holly told him, sounding chirpy, hoping to encourage him to get in his sledge and take on the challenge.

And he did.

Seeing Skye all set to slide down the fastest, longest and highest slope that was there, he jumped into his sledge without hesitation.

That was his first mistake.

Hurling two pom poms at him, the first one jolted his senses. She'd fooled him into thinking it was a real snowball. The weakener in, the second pom pom bounced off his nose.

Skye cheered. A direct hit. She couldn't have done better if she'd practised, which she hadn't. Luck and mischief were on her side.

Realising he'd been fooled by Skye the minx, Innis tried to catch up with her.

That was his second mistake.

As Innis got closer, as he was faster and more capable on the slopes than she was, she turned on the fairy lights. Her hat and scarf lit up and now she was glowing like a Christmas tree.

Was he seeing things? He blinked. No, Skye was all aglow.

Innis burst out laughing.

That was his third and worst mistake.

While Skye continued to whiz down the slope, Innis laughed his way into a snowdrift.

Skye glanced back to see Innis and his sledge skid and falter. He was out of the game.

Shame on her, she thought, for then cheering and pressing the second button on her fairy lights that made them flash on and off.

Coming to a smooth and triumphant stop at the bottom of the slope, she looked up to see Innis dust the snow from himself and pull his sledge towards her.

Her heart thundered with excitement. She'd won! Bedazzling him with the fairy lights had been the winning hand.

'Congratulations, Skye.' He smiled the cheeriest she'd ever seen him.

She smiled back at him and turned the flashing mode off. 'Thank you,' she said, still aglow.

'And here's your prize.' He dug into his jacket pocket.

'I get a trophy?' she squealed.

'No, it's a gift, an early Christmas present from me. I wanted you to have it before the ball.'

He handed her the pretty gift bag.

She peered inside it and pulled out the pink sequin evening bag. 'Oh, this is lovely. It'll match my ball gown. I love it.' Forgetting for a moment, she jumped up and hugged him.

He welcomed the gesture and hugged her close to him, or as close as he could with her pockets stuffed with pom poms.

'Sorry,' she said, unravelling herself from him.

'No, don't be.' He wanted her to feel free to hug him whenever she wanted.

Skye blushed and took the attention away from her burning cheeks by showing him the pom poms in her pockets.

'You came well–knitted out.'

She laughed. He'd made a quip. She liked this playful side of him.

'I hope it's not the best of three races because I've used up all my tricks on the first run,' she said.

'Nope. Once. You won.' He looked at the sequin bag, wishing she'd peek inside it. Never give someone a purse or a bag without popping a little something

229

inside it for luck. He'd heard this over the years, and so he'd added something special for her.

'Are you okay?' She wondered why his expression had changed. And why he kept glancing at the bag. Her reaction surely showed that she loved it.

Several others had been watching Skye's antics and came hurrying over to see what was happening.

'Fairy lights!' Rory exclaimed. 'Do I even want to know where you're hiding your batteries?'

Skye tapped her woolly hat. 'In my pom pom.'

Finlay smiled. 'When Innis said you were challenging each other, I never expected this.'

'I've got it on my phone,' Lyle announced. 'I'll send you all copies.'

'I'm going to put my gift in the car,' said Skye. 'Then we can all have fun on the slopes. No more challenges.'

Everyone had plenty of fun.

Finlay and Merrilees whizzed down the slopes, and Ean gently pushed Ailsa on her sledge giving her a start on one of the long hills. Skye and Innis waved across to Brodrick and Elspeth as they whizzed by each other, while Holly shared a slide down the slopes with Lyle. Rowen squealed as Rory took a daring dive into his sledge and slid front down all the way to the bottom of one of the fun slopes.

A mellow golden glow shaded over the day as the afternoon wore on, but by then everyone was tuckered out and ready to head home for their dinner after a great day.

Lyle drove Holly and Skye back home, along with Ailsa. Rory took Rowen with him to have dinner at his house. Finlay walked Merrilees to the nearby stargazer cottage and then headed back to the castle with Innis and Ean.

The three brothers had a lot of last minute things to attend to for the ball the following night, but everyone was looking forward to a fairytale Christmas Eve dancing the night away.

Skye and Holly changed into their cosy pyjamas and slippers, and Skye lit the fire while Holly made an easy dinner for them.

'I enjoyed the sledging,' Holly called through from the kitchen, popping a savoury vegetable pie topped with mashed potatoes from the freezer into the oven. 'Lyle has invited me to go again after Christmas.'

'I'm definitely having another run at the slopes.' Skye watched the fire spark into life and then picked up the pink sequin bag Innis had given her. The sequins glittered in the firelight. 'This bag will be a great match for my ball gown.'

'Now we know what Innis bought from Ailsa.' Holly rattled around in the kitchen, putting out the plates, cutting thick slices of bread, buttering it with butter she'd made herself from Lyle's recipe, and filling the kettle for tea.

Skye admired the shimmering sequins and then opened the bag to take a peek inside at the pink silk lining. And gasped!

'Something wrong?' Holly called to her.

'You should see what Innis has put inside my bag!' Skye's voice had notched up into a beyond excited zone.

Holly wiped her hands from buttering the bread and hurried through.

Skye held up a diamond bracelet that outshone the glittering evening bag.

'Wow!' Holly gasped too.

'I'll have to call Innis and thank him.' Skye scrambled to find where she'd put her phone. Finding it, she called him, her heart racing wildly as she fastened the bracelet on her wrist and watched the diamonds scintillate in the gold setting.

Innis was helping Finlay, Ean and Murdo organise the function room for the ball. Dinner for guests was being served in another room so that the makeshift ballroom could be decorated in Christmas grandeur.

Up a ladder, draping twinkle lights over the buffet area, assisted by Finlay, Innis took the call while balancing on the top rung.

'Skye, is everything okay?'

'A diamond bracelet!' The words were out before she could form them into a coherent sentence to thank him properly.

'Ah, you've peeked inside the bag.' He smiled, hearing the effect his gift had on her. Clearly it was the right choice.

Skye now understood why he'd been glancing at the bag when they were on the slopes. 'I didn't know you'd put another gift inside the bag,' she explained.

He told her about not giving a bag without putting something in it.

'Yes, but...wow! Just wow!'

'I wanted you to have it before the ball. When I saw it, I thought it was fit for a fairytale princess.'

She thought her heart would burst with joy. 'Lucky for you that you're at the castle because I'd squeeze the breath from you.'

'Can I have a token for that to be collected when I see you at the ball?'

'Oh, yes.' She took a steadying breath and thanked him again for the bracelet. 'But it's sooo much, Innis. Not that I don't love it. And I'm keeping it, and wearing it to the ball, just so you know.'

He laughed at her excited chatter.

'What are you up to?' she said, trying to calm down. 'I hear a bit of chaos in the background.'

'Standing on top of a high ladder adding more fairy lights to the decor for the ball.'

'You can never have too much Christmas razzle–dazzle,' she reminded him chirpily.

He mirrored her question. 'What are you up to?'

'I'm dazzled by diamonds and about to have dinner by the fire.'

'Sounds cosy.'

'It is. And very, very sparkly.'

On a happy note they ended the call so Innis could get on with lighting up the function room ready for the ball.

CHAPTER SIXTEEN

The vintage dress shop mannequin seemed to be putting up a struggle as Skye tried to get her pink ball gown off it from the window display. It was late afternoon and they'd changed the shop sign from open to *closed until after Christmas*.

Holly stepped into the window to help her, and together they wrestled the ball gown and the mannequin into submission.

'Phew!' Skye sighed. 'That was tricky. I didn't want to pull the dress in case I ripped it or dislodged the sequins.'

Holly tried not to laugh.

'Giggle if you want,' said Skye, starting to smile.

'The mannequin wasn't letting go without a fight,' said Holly, putting an evening dress on it while Skye fluffed out the layers of pink organza on her ball gown.

Holly's amber and gold gown was hanging on a rail ready to be worn.

'I don't know about you, but I'm buzzing with excitement.' Skye sounded full of nervous energy which she was sure she'd dance off at the ball. All that waltzing while trying to keep in step and not trip over her dress was a lot to juggle, but she'd been watching videos showing how to dance while wearing a full–skirted dress.

Checking that everything was secure, they wrapped their dresses up carefully, turned the shop lights off, locked the door and drove up the hill to their house to get ready for the ball.

Lyle looked immaculate in his black dinner suit. He adjusted his black bow tie as he got out of his car to help Holly and Skye into the vehicle dressed in their finery.

'You both look like princesses.' Lyle's compliment was genuine.

They wore vintage opera coats over their ball gowns. Skye's coat was light pink and silver brocade, while Holly's was gold brocade.

Their hair and makeup suited their individual styling, and Skye played up her wide blue eyes with lashings of mascara and soft pink lipstick. Holly emphasised her eyes with bronze and gold that went well with her amber and gold dress, and her chestnut hair was pinned up into a classy chignon. Skye's long, strawberry blonde locks were pinned up at the sides but she kept the length around her shoulders and tumbling down her back. Both wore their tiara hair bands and clutched their evening bags.

The diamond bracelet was hidden under the long sleeves of Skye's opera coat, but was due to be revealed when she arrived at the castle.

They'd opted to wear court shoes with lower heels for dancing, and these were in gold and pink to match their dresses.

Innis had offered to come down and give Skye a lift to the castle, but as he was one of the main hosts of the event, Skye had decided to go with Lyle and Holly.

The chatter in the car on the drive up to the castle was cheery, and only a few flakes of snow fluttered down from the clear night sky as Lyle parked in the castle's busy car park.

The front entrance glowed in welcoming and the light from inside poured out into the snow–covered garden. The magnificent castle was aglow with lights and festive decorations extended out to the large Christmas tree outside the building and fairy lights were entwined through the greenery that was sprinkled with snow.

Music filtered out, and numerous people were arriving for the special event.

Lyle jumped out of the car and helped Holly and Skye step out into the cold night. Luckily, the snow had called a truce to allow guests to walk in without facing a blizzard.

Innis ran out from the doorway to escort Skye and welcomed all three of them inside. He wore his black and dark grey kilt with a white shirt, tie, waistcoat and cropped black jacket. His sporran was attached to his belt by a silver chain, and a skean dhu was tucked into his thick woollen socks that he wore with brogues.

The billowing opera coats hid their ball gowns, and it was only when Innis and Lyle helped Skye and Holly off with their coats near reception where they were carefully checked–in to the cloakroom by staff, that the full beauty of their gowns emerged.

Innis was silent for a moment, his heart reacting to Skye standing there smiling happily at him. Her sparkling pink ball gown and tiara hair band made her look like a fairytale princess.

Lyle acted likewise when he saw Holly wearing the amber and gold ball gown and tiara hair band.

'Shall we go through?' Innis said to Skye, offering her his arm to rest her hand as they entered the function room. The doors were open wide leading into the ballroom–size suite. The Christmas decorations and chandeliers added to the opulence of the room.

The buffet spread along one wall was already busy with guests helping themselves to the festive fayre, but no one was yet up dancing.

Ailsa, wearing her royal blue gown and tiara head band was there with Ean, chatting to Merrilees in her ice blue ball gown. Finlay was standing at her side, and noticed Innis nodding over to him. A signal they'd pre–planned.

'Would you like to dance with me, Skye?' Innis held out his hand to her.

Glancing at the empty floor, Skye saw that Ailsa and Merrilees were taking to the floor with Ean and Finlay.

'I'd love to,' Skye told him, more excited than nervous as the music changed to a festive waltz.

The three brothers as hosts, then beckoned Lyle and Holly, Rory and Rowen, and others to join in.

Soon, the dance floor was busy with couples waltzing around in their ball gowns, kilts and evening suits to the music.

Murdo smiled at Geneen. 'Shall we?'

Geneen, wearing her new deep blue gown, was happy to dance with Murdo.

Rory wore a classic dinner suit, white shirt and tie, and his ruffled blond hair had been tamed and slicked back. Clasping Rowen's hand, he walked with her on to the dance floor and they began to waltz around with the others. Rowen's dress was a confection of cream and gold sparkle and her hair was pinned up in a chignon.

All the ladies wore tiara style head bands or glittering clasps in their hair, raising the bar for their evening at the fairytale ball.

A couple of their farmer friends accompanied Rosabel and Primrose. They'd both restyled their pink and yellow ball gowns and joined in the dancing.

'You look beautiful, Skye,' Innis told her as they waltzed around.

'Thank you again for the bracelet.' It sparkled on her wrist.

'Would you like to get something to eat from the buffet?' he offered.

'Yes, I haven't had dinner.'

Escorting her over to the buffet, they helped themselves to the various delicacies, as did other guests. Nairne had created a buffet catering for a wide range of tastes. The savoury selection, especially the mini quiche, made from Lyle's recipe, were enjoyed along with Scottish salmon dishes and turkey with all the trimmings. Lyle had contributed cakes and his Yule logs, and Brodrick's ice cream was proving to be popular. Innis' cakes and chocolates were part of the buffet menu too.

Chatting to friends and acquaintances, Skye felt what it would be like to be with Innis, as a couple, and she liked how it made her feel.

When they'd finished eating, Innis's eyes sparked with the type of mischief Skye often saw in herself.

'Are you feeling daring?' Innis whispered to her.

Skye looked up at him. 'Daring?'

'Yes.' There was a challenge in his tone.

Skye picked up on it and was now intrigued. 'What did you have in mind?'

'Come with me,' said Innis. 'We won't be long. Then we'll come back down for the dancing.'

'*Back* down? Where are you taking me?'

Innis clasped her hand and hurried away with her while her heady giggles trailed behind her.

He took her up the private staircase, along the corridor, past his suite, and stopped at the door leading up to one of the turrets.

'Hold tight to me and close your eyes.' He picked her up and she put her arms around his shoulders as he ran up the stairs of the turret and emerged through a doorway on the roof.

Trusting him, even when she felt the cold air against her bare arms and shoulders, she snuggled into him and kept her eyes shut.

She felt him place her down gently while keeping his protective arms around her.

'Okay, you can look now.'

Skye blinked as she opened her eyes and saw that they were standing in a private but secure part of the castle's rooftop. The view of the castle's estate, the forest, the sea shimmering like silver in the distance, looked magical.

The vast sky arched overhead and was scattered with stars, with one bright star outshining them all high above them.

'You're quite safe. We need access to the roof, but stay close to me.'

He saw her shiver, from excitement, the thrill of where they were, and the icy air. Taking his jacket off, he draped it over her shoulders and wrapped his arms around her.

She pressed her back against his strong chest and gazed in awe at the view of the island. 'It's like a fairytale,' she murmured.

'It is. Our fairytale.'

She smiled and leaned back into him, looking up at the glittering stars. 'That's the North Star. It's the brightest one.'

'You once told me that you'd wished upon it,' he confided. 'And I decided to make a wish on it too.'

'You made a wish on the North Star?' She tilted her head to look round at him.

'I did. Ean encouraged me—'

'Ean encouraged you to wish on the star?' she cut–in. 'I thought it was only Holly and me that did things like that.'

'You inspired me to try.'

His words warmed her heart.

'Are we allowed another wish, or have we both used up our quota?' he said.

'I think we have, but we could make a wish together,' she suggested.

'I know what I want to wish for.' His tone sounded full of love for her.

'So do I.'

'Let's make our wish and hope it comes true,' he said.

Gazing up at the North Star they silently made their wishes, that were the same if only they'd known — to have a happy and loving life together.

Skye couldn't help but shiver in the freezing cold breeze that blew through her hair. Her tiara hair band kept the stray strands away from her beautiful face.

Innis turned her around and looked at her. Those amber eyes were lighter, filled with love for Skye. 'I have to tell you that I've fallen in love with you,' he said.

'I've fallen in love with you too.'

He leaned down and kissed her.

'We'd better get back to the ball before they send out a search party,' he joked.

Letting him lift her again, she clung close as he walked to the doorway and down the turret stairs. He should've put her down in the upstairs hallway, but Skye's rascal elements were rubbing off on him, and he walked down the staircase leading to reception, causing quite a stir.

He finally placed her down at the doorway of the function room.

'Where were you two?' said Finlay.

'Getting a breath of fresh air.' Innis' reply made Skye smile, and she squeezed his arm as she linked hers through his.

Innis swept her on to the dance floor and they waltzed around under the chandeliers and twinkling fairy lights.

The sparkle on the fabric of Skye's dress glittered under the lighting as she danced with Innis. The organza felt as light as air and the sequins and crystals on the bodice reflected on her lovely pale skin. She'd always imagined what it would be like to dance at a ball. The experience outshone her dreams, especially as she was waltzing around with Innis. He looked so handsome in his full dress kilt wear, and although she'd managed to dance in the ball gown without faltering, she felt his strong arms guide her smoothly.

Skye saw that it was snowing outside as they waltzed by the windows that had a view of the castle's back garden and forest estate beyond. It created the perfect atmosphere as they danced.

She smiled at Holly and Lyle dancing by, pleased that her sister had found romance this Christmas.

Enjoying the dancing and the buffet until after midnight, the evening finally came to a close with a slow dance.

'I'm looking forward to having Christmas Day here tomorrow,' Skye told Innis as he held her close.

'It's officially after midnight, so you know what that means,' he said.

Skye frowned.

Innis leaned down and kissed her. 'Merry Christmas, Skye.'

She felt his kiss linger. 'Merry Christmas, Innis.'

A few of their friends smiled, noticing the love between them, nothing hidden. Skye and Innis were clearly a couple in love.

As the ball finally came to an end, people filtered out of the castle and headed home.

Innis walked Skye to Lyle's car. Lyle accompanied Holly.

'I had a wonderful evening,' Skye told Innis. She glanced up at the castle's turret where they'd shared their feelings on the roof. It was their secret, for now, but she doubted she'd be able to keep such a magical moment to herself for long.

Innis smiled at her. 'I'll see you for Christmas at the castle.'

Driving Skye and Holly away, they all waved to Innis as he stood there in his kilt with the snow falling all around him, backed by the glow of the magnificent fairytale castle.

Christmas morning in Skye and Holly's house was filled with squeals of delight as they exchanged presents. Still in their pyjamas and slippers, they sat near the Christmas tree and opened each gift with as much excitement as they'd had since they were little.

Makeup, perfume, hand knitted items and an extra sewing box for Skye were included along with a few vintage items such as a fifties vanity set for Holly.

As the invitation to have Christmas Day at the castle had been a last minute gesture, Innis had told them that no gifts were required. But Skye and Holly had plans to spoil Innis and Lyle with hand knitted jumpers, hats and scarves that they were going to make for them soon.

The morning flew in and they got ready for Lyle picking them up. They were due to arrive at the castle around lunchtime. They'd brought their dresses with them from the shop the previous day. Skye had decided to wear the pink brocade dress and Holly opted for the red velvet.

'You look lovely in that pink brocade,' said Holly.

'And your red velvet dress is so Christmassy.'

Holly smoothed her hands down the soft velvet. 'Can I borrow your red wool coat?'

'Yes, I'm wearing my cream one.'

Holly heard a car pull up outside and peeked out the window. 'That's Lyle.'

Grabbing their coats and bags, they hurried out to the car.

Lyle wore a smart suit and as always, the drive to the castle was cheery. Lyle had secret gifts for Holly that he planned to give her privately later — a top of the range food mixer that was great for baking, and a vintage floral teapot like the ones in his tea shop she'd admired.

Christmas Day dinner at the castle was traditional. Innis, Finlay and Ean welcomed their guests to join them at their private table near the Christmas tree. The warmth from the fire added to the festive ambience.

'You look beautiful, as always,' Innis whispered to Skye as everyone exchanged Christmas hugs and handshakes.

Skye was seated beside Innis and throughout the meal they chatted to each other and to those around the table. It was a Christmas to remember, Skye thought, at times sitting back and taking in the romance and friendship of the day.

'Do you usually celebrate Christmas like this?' Skye said to Innis.

'Usually our parents are home and we celebrate here like a family along with the guests,' he said. 'But this year there's romance to celebrate along with Christmas.'

Dancing was once again part of the festivities, and although Skye mainly danced with Innis, everyone danced with everyone else, and Christmas ceilidh dances were thrown into the mix as befitted the Scottish castle.

'Wheee!' Skye squealed linking arms with Innis and then Finlay. She was glad she'd worn her comfy court shoes so that she could keep up with the whirling and twirling.

Innis wore his kilt, though not the full kilted finery from the ball, but still quite formal. As the day wore on, he took his jacket off, and his white ghillie shirt that laced up the front displayed his strong chest, especially after the lively ceilidh dancing.

In a group photo that Murdo took of them all and then shared with them, Skye saw herself fit into Innis' world. Her heart squeezed just looking at the lone wolf who didn't want to be alone any longer. Snatched moments throughout Christmas Day and into the evening, enabled Innis to reveal that his intentions weren't like those of his brothers when it came to romance — and getting engaged. Skye always felt she had a mind of her own, and though mercurial in character, her instincts never let her down. Everything that Innis suggested suited her perfectly.

Marriage would be on the cards at an appropriate time, though it seemed that they'd tie the knot before Finlay and Merrilees and Ean and Ailsa. Again, nothing jarred Skye's senses with this plan. Her parents had met and married within a short time of meeting and had enjoyed a long and happy marriage, something she longed for too. Besides, she'd known Innis for a while now.

'The future is what we make it,' Innis whispered to her as they stood beside the Christmas tree gazing out at the snow.

'Yes, it is,' Skye agreed, feeling a heady mix of excitement and romance.

Watching the snow falling outside the castle windows, Skye felt that her future was here with him. She would still have her shop with Holly. Nothing would change her love for vintage fashion. And Innis would continue with his cake shop, adding the extension and enjoying his chocolatier work.

'Would you like to dance with me before I drive you home?' said Innis.

'Yes.'

They danced to a popular Christmas song from the past, and then Innis escorted her outside into the cold night, helped her into his car, and drove her back down to the coast.

This allowed Lyle and Holly to have some private time as he drove her home.

Skye glanced back at the castle, smiling at the wonderful Christmastime she'd had there.

The trees that bordered the forest road were covered in white frost and sprinkled with snowflakes that glittered in the starlight.

Innis pulled the car over for a few minutes so they could admire the view of the wintry sea. All along the coast, and the curve of the bay down by the harbour and main street, was covered in snow.

'The snow falling over the sea looks magical,' said Skye.

'I've always thought that too. I love this island.' Innis leaned close and kissed Skye. Then they snuggled close for a while, watching the snow and the sea before he dropped her off home.

During the next couple of days, more sledging was enjoyed on the slopes by Skye, Innis and the others.

Then it was time for Innis to reopen his cake shop, and although Skye and Holly kept their dress shop shut for a few days longer, the shops and businesses in the main street sparked back into busy mode. Lyle reopened his tea shop and Holly spent quite a bit of time there learning new recipes with him.

At the end of a busy day at the cake shop, Innis wrapped up warm, locked the cake shop and strode up the hill in the snowy twilight.

The only footprints on the hilltop were his. He breathed in the crisp, fresh winter air, and gazed out at his favourite view of the island.

He could see the lights glittering along the main street. And there was his cake shop, aglow with the night display lights illuminating the cakes and chocolates in the window.

The vintage dress shop was still unlit, but he pictured Skye sitting cosy by the fire at home knitting. She'd shown him the classic pattern for the cream Aran knit jumper she was knitting for him. Perhaps he'd see her later, or let her relax snug by the fireside.

Gazing out at the view, the breeze blew through his hair, refreshing his energy after the hectic day. There was something invigorating about locking up his shop for the evening and bounding up the hill to see the view he never got tired of.

The scent of the snow mixed with the sea air. He breathed it all in.

Before leaving, he took a long, lingering look at his favourite view of the island.

Whack!

A snowball hit off the side of his shoulder.

Innis heard the impish giggling before he glanced round at the figure challenging him to a snowball fight.

Skye, wrapped up warm against the winter's night, wearing the pink woolly hat without the fairy lights, had another snowball in her mitts.

'Why you little scallywag!' Innis shouted, trying not to laugh.

Seeing the humorous but hunter's look in those wolf eyes, Skye made a run for it to avoid being caught.

'Yes, you'd better run, Skye.' His voice sounded deep in the cold air. 'You know what will happen when I catch you.'

'Promises, promises,' she shouted as she ran away.

Her furry boots slowed her down. That was her excuse. But within moments Innis caught her, swept her up in his strong arms, swung her around and then placed her down gently. He kept his arms around her though. He wasn't letting her go, not ever.

248

'I promise I'll always love you,' he said, gazing at her with love–light in his eyes. 'I promise never to break your heart.'

'Those are promises I'll hold you to,' she said, smiling up at him.

Innis leaned down and kissed her, sealing the promises he'd made.

Then they stood together gazing out at their favourite view of the island. He stood behind her, his arms wrapped around her shoulders, shielding her from the cold breeze. Skye leaned back against him, and looked out at the snow covering the island, the hill, the countryside, the sea and the little shops in the main street, seeing their future together.

And there, shining bright in the twilight sky, was the North Star.

They smiled as they stood close, happy that both of their wishes had come true during their fairytale Christmas on the island.

End

About the Author:

De-ann Black is a bestselling author, scriptwriter and former newspaper journalist. She has over 100 books published. Romance, thrillers, espionage novels, action adventure. And children's books (non-fiction rocket science books and children's fiction). She became an Amazon All-Star author in 2014 and 2015.

She previously worked as a full-time newspaper journalist for several years. She had her own weekly columns in the press. This included being a motoring correspondent where she got to test drive cars every week for the press for three years.

Before being asked to work for the press, De-ann worked in magazine editorial writing everything from fashion features to social news. She was the marketing editor of a glossy magazine.

She is also a professional artist and illustrator. Embroidery design, fabric design, dressmaking, sewing, knitting and fashion are part of her work.

Additionally, De-ann has always been interested in fitness, and was a fitness and bodybuilding champion, 100 metre runner and mountaineer. As a former N.A.B.B.A. Miss Scotland, she had a weekly fitness show on the radio that ran for over three years.

De-ann trained in Shukokai karate, boxing, kickboxing, Dayan Qigong and Jiu Jitsu. She is currently based in Scotland.

Her 16 colouring books are available in paperback, including her latest Summer Nature Colouring Book and Flower Nature Colouring Book.

Her latest embroidery pattern books include: Floral Garden Embroidery Patterns, Christmas & Winter Embroidery Patterns, Floral Spring Embroidery Patterns and Sea Theme Embroidery Patterns.

Website: Find out more at: www.de-annblack.com

Fabric, Wallpaper & Home Decor Collections:
De-ann's fabric designs and wallpaper collections, and home decor items, including her popular Scottish Garden Thistles patterns, are available from Spoonflower.
www.de-annblack.com/spoonflower

Also by De-ann Black (Romance, Action/Thrillers & Children's books). See her Amazon Author page or website for further details about her books, screenplays, illustrations, art, fabric designs and embroidery patterns.

Amazon Author page:
www.De-annBlack.com/Amazon

Romance books:

The Cure for Love Romance series:
1. The Cure for Love
2. The Cure for Love at Christmas

Scottish Highlands & Island Romance series:
1. Scottish Island Knitting Bee
2. Scottish Island Fairytale Castle
3. Vintage Dress Shop on the Island
4. Fairytale Christmas on the Island

Scottish Loch Romance series:
1. Sewing & Mending Cottage
2. Scottish Loch Summer Romance

Quilting Bee & Tea Shop series:
1. The Quilting Bee
2. The Tea Shop by the Sea
3. Embroidery Cottage
4. Knitting Shop by the Sea
5. Christmas Weddings

Sewing, Crafts & Quilting series:
1. The Sewing Bee
2. The Sewing Shop
3. Knitting Cottage (Scottish Highland romance)
4. Scottish Highlands Christmas Wedding
(Embroidery, Knitting, Dressmaking & Textile Art)

Cottages, Cakes & Crafts series:
1. The Flower Hunter's Cottage
2. The Sewing Bee by the Sea
3. The Beemaster's Cottage
4. The Chocolatier's Cottage
5. The Bookshop by the Seaside
6. The Dressmaker's Cottage

Scottish Chateau, Colouring & Crafts series:
1. Christmas Cake Chateau
2. Colouring Book Cottage

Snow Bells Haven series:
1. Snow Bells Christmas
2. Snow Bells Wedding

Summer Sewing Bee

Sewing, Knitting & Baking series:
1. The Tea Shop
2. The Sewing Bee & Afternoon Tea
3. The Christmas Knitting Bee
4. Champagne Chic Lemonade Money
5. The Vintage Sewing & Knitting Bee

The Tea Shop & Tearoom series:
1. The Christmas Tea Shop & Bakery
2. The Christmas Chocolatier
3. The Chocolate Cake Shop in New York at Christmas
4. The Bakery by the Seaside
5. Shed in the City

Tea Dress Shop series:
1. The Tea Dress Shop At Christmas
2. The Fairytale Tea Dress Shop In Edinburgh
3. The Vintage Tea Dress Shop In Summer

Christmas Romance series:
1. Christmas Romance in Paris
2. Christmas Romance in Scotland

Oops! I'm the Paparazzi series:
1. Oops! I'm the Paparazzi
2. Oops! I'm Up To Mischief
3. Oops! I'm the Paparazzi, Again

The Bitch-Proof Suit series:
1. The Bitch-Proof Suit
2. The Bitch-Proof Romance
3. The Bitch-Proof Bride
4. The Bitch-Proof Wedding

Heather Park: Regency Romance
Dublin Girl
Why Are All The Good Guys Total Monsters?
I'm Holding Out For A Vampire Boyfriend

Action/Thriller books:

Knight in Miami

Agency Agenda

Love Him Forever

Someone Worse

Electric Shadows

The Strife Of Riley

Shadows Of Murder

Cast a Dark Shadow

Children's books:

Faeriefied

Secondhand Spooks

Poison-Wynd

Wormhole Wynd

Science Fashion

School For Aliens

Colouring books:

Summer Nature

Flower Nature

Summer Garden

Spring Garden

Autumn Garden

Sea Dream

Festive Christmas

Christmas Garden

Christmas Theme

Flower Bee

Wild Garden

Faerie Garden Spring

Flower Hunter

Stargazer Space

Bee Garden

Scottish Garden

Seasons

Embroidery Design books:

Sea Theme Embroidery Patterns

Floral Garden Embroidery Patterns

Christmas & Winter Embroidery Patterns

Floral Spring Embroidery Patterns

Floral Nature Embroidery Designs

Scottish Garden Embroidery Designs

Printed in Great Britain
by Amazon

32075731R00145